THE BATTLE OF....

BLACK JACK

'56

It didn't start at Ft. Sumter !

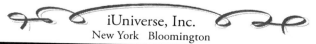

iUniverse, Inc.
New York   Bloomington

D1519282

Black Jack '56
The First Battle of the American Civil War

The character of Abrael Kepper is fictitious as is the Potter family. All other names, dates and places are historically correct according to the research available to the Author. Conversations are either exact or implied by the historical circumstances at the time. Source material available and can be provided by the Author upon request.

Book cover design © Dale E. Vaughn

iUniverse books may be ordered through booksellers or by contacting:

iUniverse
1663 Liberty Drive
Bloomington, IN 47403
www.iuniverse.com
1-800-Authors (1-800-288-4677)

ISBN: 978-1-4401-8308-9 (sc)
ISBN: 978-1-4401-8309-6 (ebk)

1. Historical novel – Kansas – Fiction
2. Kansas – Kansas Territory
3. American Civil War
4. John Brown – Pottawatomie Massacre
5. Historical fact and fiction

Printed in the United States of America
iUniverse rev. date: 05/24/2010

Dedication

To
KATHARINE KELLEY
1910 – 2005

Baldwin City teacher and historian who
watched over her part of the
Santa Fe Trail
and who's grandparent's home was
burned by Quantrill in 1863.

*"I had over 2,000 children but
never married."*

The Historical Novel

Although a full time resident of Kansas my interest in its history didn't come about until one day a number of years ago when I was made aware that the first Black troops to fight in the American Civil War came from Kansas. And, I had heard the term "Bloody Kansas" many times but the real significance hadn't registered.

I was invited by a friend to attend a meeting of the Topeka Civil War Round Table and that's what did it. It seemed like over night I became aware that Kansas had a very large part in the beginning of that terrible tragedy. I had to know more and right away. This was my State.

My need to know the facts and relate them in written form began at that point. I wanted others to know that Kansas was not just a place with a few cowboys that helps fill in between the Mississippi and the Rockies. Kansas is a very important part of our history. It isn't that I always want to know everything, as my wife sometimes says, but I if it is something I care about I want to know the **real facts** and *why*!

Because I now speak to many groups about Kansas History I have often been asked if I am a teacher or history professor. I answer that I am definitely not a teacher but a story teller. In the words of the late Shelby Foote *"we need more writers and fewer historians; "historians don't know how to write, to make the facts come alive"*.

To prepare for ***"The Chance",*** my book about the First Kansas Colored Volunteer Infantry**,** I walked every battle field at which *my guys* fought. At some locations I believed I could feel their presence urging me to tell the real story; not just of the battles but of how they felt and why they were willing to risk their lives for white folks that didn't even want to associate with them, much less risk their lives next to them on a battle field.

That is when I discovered I loved to do research. Digging and finding out things either little known or generally passed over is a thrill to me. Such was the case when I discovered the court testimony concerning the Pottawatomie massacre. It had always been there but everyone either ignored it or didn't notice it at all tucked away in a couple of letters written by some of the participants.

I first learned about Black Jack as the result of a meeting with a small group of folks from Baldwin City, Kansas. They were just a few citizens aware of the battle about three miles east of their city and the significance of that encounter between a Free-State and a pro-slavery militia; North against the South, over whether the Kansas Territory would become a free or a slave state. It was that simple and that direct. What lead up to the battle and what followed was the beginning of one of the worst times in the life of our country; a time when Americans fought each other!

Interview with Shelby Foote noted historical novelist, 1994.
    "…..I have a strong belief that novelists have a great deal to teach historians about plotting, about character drawing, about other things, especially learning to be a good writer which most historians don't bother to do...about dramatic composition which I consider the best history to be." Aristotle said in criticizing great drama,

> '*first you must learn how to write well,*
> *then you learn how to draw characters*
> *that can stand up and cast a shadow,*
> *then you learn to plot.*'

That is the skill that comes last if it comes at all. And that is where I think historians neglect a huge advantage. History has a plot, you don't make it up, you discover it; it is there."

Shelby Foote   **Author of "Civil War" Vol. I, II, III**

THE FACTS!

While the character of Abrael is fictitious and some of the conversations are what I feel fitting at the time, the facts remain unaltered along with the very real spirit of the day and times. Only the truth offered herein can help make clear the awful experience the people of Kansas endured.

Honest, accurate and true history is the skeleton; the novelist puts the meat on the bones to make it come alive. I hope this part of Kansas history comes alive for you, the reader.

Dale E. Vaughn

FOREWORD

In addition to **The Battle of Black Jack** this book is probably just as much about the **Pottawatomie Massacre**, the **Wakarusa War** and especially the **Kansas-Nebraska Act**.

Passed on May 30, 1854, the **K-B** act could easily be considered the *"first shot"* fired to begin what became the American Civil War.

Prior to the enactment of that bill, it was generally accepted that the Missouri Compromise of 1820 had pretty much settled the question of if and how the spread of slavery would continue. Yet it was so controversial and troubling that even Thomas Jefferson feared the results. He wrote in a letter dated April 22, 1820, to his friend John Holms that *"...like a fire bell in the night, awakened and filled me with terror. I considered it at once as the knell of the Union"*. The bill passed and was good for thirty years. Then the Compromise of 1850 combined with the Fugitive Slave Act for all intents and purposes repealed the Compromise of 1820.

Still, slavery would be allowed in any state that would be formed south of the *southern border* of the State of Missouri. That would include the territories of Arizona, New Mexico, Nevada and Utah, not really prime plantation type real estate. And it would be a matter of *let the people decide:* **"POPULAR SOVEREIGNTY"**; not really a new idea of Stephen Douglas'.

Surprisingly, a chance of opening up Kansas and Nebraska didn't seem to settle well with either North or South. With the South, it was the popular sovereignty thing again; running the risk that there would be enough people to opt for a free state. The North was afraid of an outside chance the slavers might win the new State if the Missourians had their way. The North was willing to allow slavery to die out on its own if it stayed in the South and the South knew that is exactly what would happen if they were not allowed to grow along with the Northern Free States. When it was realized that the enormous territory north and west of Missouri's southern border was larger than the entire south put together, that really started the panic in Missouri and the rest of the South.

Southerners, who had no real knowledge of what the Kansas Territory was like, assumed that since it was right next to Missouri it would be very much like Missouri. That meant a huge amount of available slave territory filled with tobacco, cotton and hemp that might work for them at least half way to the Rocky Mountains. So here came the pro-slavery people by the hundreds, determined to bring their votes and slaves to a much needed addition to southern culture. And it would mean that there would be the chance of continued equal representation in Washington City.

It was accepted that Nebraska would stay free because it certainly wasn't tobacco or cotton land and no real need for large amounts of slaves to work the land. The Northerners could have that.

There was no denying that there were more Americans against allowing slavery to grow than there were those that were either pro-slavery or just didn't care. Many of these folks knew that Kansas was a different kind of farm land so they began to pour in from the northeast ready to cast their ballots for freedom for everyone willing to work for it. They looked upon the Kansas-Nebraska Act as their chance for not only a new start in the West but at the same time an opportunity to stop or at least slow down the growth of slavery.

But it was soon realized; it wasn't going to happen without a fight!

Dale E. Vaughn

BLACK JACK '56

The First Battle of the American Civil War

Prologue

Monday June 2, 1856

   "A man could get hisef killed bein' here."

   "It's less likely if you keep movin' and keep your head down."

   "I can't figure out jes why y'all people are here in this mess anyhow."

   "Well…we've been fighting for a place for our-selves as far back as our history goes. Why should this be any different? Besides, you never know, this could be a turning point. We might find at least a small piece of ground here to call our own."

   "Sounds t' me like a funny place for y'all folks to come to. Sure, wouldn't think a bunch of Jews would end up in a place like Kansas."

Chapter 1

Spring, 1853

"Are you certain you want to go to such a place? That country west of Missouri is all wild Indian country."

"But Sir, it won't always be wild. I hear that is going to change and it is said that people are going to be moving west and land will soon be available just past the western Missouri border."

John Potter waved away the remark. "Look; there must be over fifteen different Indian tribes out there and I wager none of them are anxious to share their land with anyone. It's one thing crossing their land to get to Utah or Oregon but to try to take away their lands…? They have been moved and shoved around much like we have and they aren't going to put up with more of that kind of treatment.

"Abrael, I believe you are just asking for more grief. And to be quite frank, on top of everything you must remember you are Jewish. Don't you have enough worries as it is?"

"But, maybe out there it won't matter," Abrael said quickly. "Maybe they will be different out there."

"And just what kind of folks do you think you will find *out there*, as you call it?"

"Well…"

"Remember Abrael, those people out there are the same as the ones here because they came from places just like this and like back where you grew up. Just changing a location isn't going to change a mind about such things."

"I appreciate your concern Mr. Potter but you must remember we Jews have been fighting for a place of our own for hundreds of years. We can't just keep to ourselves or keep running trying to avoid conflict." Abrael Kepper looked at Mr. Potter and then shifted his gaze to his hands folded in his lap.

"You mean you don't think leaving for the western country is not running away?" asked Mr. Potter in a somewhat raised voice. "Just why would you be better off there than here? In my estimation you are just trading a fairly simple life here for more problems and in a place you know very little about."

"Well, I…"

"Abrael, we are Mormons. We know about persecution and what it is like to be run out of a place we call home. But now that we have settled here in Missouri, I believe we can be accepted and left alone to work our farm and tend to our family."

Mr. Potter stood up and walked toward the window then turned and looked at Abrael. "This can be your home too. We want you to stay. You are like one of our own. Jeremy thinks the world of you and you have helped him so much I believe you are fond of him too. Please reconsider."

"Mr. Potter, I am very grateful to you and the others. And you are right; you have treated me as one of the family. It has meant a great deal to me to have a home and to be able to feel that Jeremy is like a brother, but…"

"But your mind is made up, right?"

"I must find and build a home for myself, Mr. Potter. And I do know about that part of the country. I know there is free farm land and that soon it will be a territory and then a State and the people will decide for themselves whether it will be free or slave."

"You really think they will let them do that, Abrael?"

"Maybe they will, and maybe I can help make it happen.

"There for the first time I'll have a part in deciding what my home will be like." Abrael took a quick breath and continued. "I want to be a teacher and help people. Out there, in the new land, with new communities, I can do that and be on my own and live my own way."

"You can do that here, Abrael. You have proved that with Jeremy and several of the other children in the community," Mr. Potter insisted.

"Father," said Mrs. Potter who had been silent during the conversation, "The boy wants to make his own way. Someday it will be the same with Jeremy and the other children. We must let him do what he thinks is best." Mrs. Potter smiled lovingly at Abrael, "He is a grown man. We must help, not discourage."

"All right, look. If you must go," stated Mr. Potter, "why not go on up into the Oregon Territory or even the new Washington Territory? And we have friends in the Utah Territory who will give you some help on the way if you need it."

"That is a thought," agreed Mrs. Potter. "Now that Brigham Young is governor of the Utah Territory the new city of Salt Lake is beginning to flourish. We hear it is a beautiful valley and you might even decide to stay."

"I'm not certain the Mormons would welcome a young Jew to their new home," said Abrael, half jokingly.

"If ya decide to stay," chimed in the youthful Jeremy Potter, with a large grin on his face, "you could have yourself two or three pretty young wives. They're doin' that out there now."

"Now you just hush that kind of talk young man," said Jeremy's mother. Then with a sly glance at her husband she said, "you'll be giving your father ideas."

"What? Why no such thing," stammered Mr. Potter. "I've never said that I agree with…."

"Any way," interrupted Abrael, trying to get back to their original discussion, "who knows? I might decide to go on. We'll see."

Abrael Kepper, Jewish, twenty-one years old, only occasionally referred to as Abe, had, as Mr. Potter said, made up his mind. It was time for him to be on his own. He had given up his dream of becoming a rabbi because there was no place he could learn all that would be necessary to fulfill such a position but he could continue to be as good a Jew as he knew how and he could become a teacher. After all that would practically be the same thing...well in a way, he thought. He knew he would miss the Potters, who as Mr. Potter had said had become as a family to Abrael.

Abrael had been born in Newport, Rhode Island July 31, 1832. His family had immigrated there many years ago from a settlement in the Dutch West Indies. The Dutch had more tolerance for the Jews than did the French or the Spanish. In the islands, Jews had settled an area named Jodenwyk and a congregation had been established in Willemstad; the Sephardic Congregation named Mikveh Israel. The then tiny settlement in New Port, Rhode Island, of which Abrael's forefathers had been a part, had been sponsored and assisted by the Curacao congregation.

Rhode Island seemed like the perfect place for the Jews to go since a number of other groups had settled there for religious freedom beginning when Roger Williams welcomed Anne Hutchins and her husband who had been banished from the Massachusetts Bay colony in 1637. Williams himself had fled Salem for religious reasons and had been greeted and accepted by the Narragansett Indians in 1636.

Abrael's parents died in 1847 when Abrael was fifteen, leaving him alone, having no brothers or sisters. It seemed the general attitude of the public had become less tolerant since the Narragansetts left and Abrael was accepted by very few due to his religion. He was, however, befriended by the Potter family who was on their way west due also to being less than welcome since they were Mormons. The Potters managed to obtain a small farm close to the Meramec River in central Missouri and sank their roots. "I'll not be moved from my home again," stated Mr. Potter firmly.

Recently Abrael had been uneasy without really knowing why. He had a good life with the Potters and he was able, at least to a small extent, to realize his desire to be a teacher. Abrael had always liked books and he would sit by the hour listing to the stories told by his grandfather and the elders of their community. He learned much about his heritage and the history of his people and seemed never to be able to quench his thirst for knowledge. His father had been told that Abrael, his mother would never allow him to be called Abe, that Abrael was very quick of mind and would do well in business. Abrael, however, had no desire to go into any kind of business except teaching in one form or another.

Now it was time. It wasn't just the warm spring weather that made something stir within him. Now he knew why he was restless and dissatisfied. Finally Abrael knew he had a real purpose for his life.

He had saved some of the money he received for tutoring assignments from affluent families such as Mr. John Webber and several others who were planning to send their son or daughter to school back east. His constant studying and reading had prepared him with a pretty good educational background. He had also done odd jobs for some of the other farmers and vineyard owners. He had done some work for Lt. James Abert who was surveying for a new railroad in the area. The Potters would not accept any money for Abrael staying with them, saying the work he did around the farm and helping Jeremy was all the contribution he needed to make. After all, he was just like family.

He would give himself about a year to save what more he could and solidify his plans. Then he would make his move; just as the weather broke early next spring. He would march off into the wilderness just as his ancestors had done hundreds of years ago. He would go but not just to wander aimlessly for the rest of his life. He would go, find his place and establish himself. He had the confidence and fearlessness of the young. With God's help he was certain he would succeed!

He… he hoped.

A. Lincoln

Courtesy Kansas Historical Society

Chapter 2

Sunday June 11, 1854

In preparing for his journey into a new life in the Kansas Territory, Abrael was well aware of the potential political controversy and possibly even turmoil that could occur before the territory would finally become a State.

He had followed, in the St. Louis newspapers, the accounts of the actions in Washington City and knew he could not help but be drawn into whatever difficulties the new settlers could encounter. He had given much thought to his role in helping to build not only a new home and life for himself but that of a new and hopefully Free State.

Abrael was not alone in his concern about the future of the Kansas Territory. A forty-five year old traveling lawyer, currently making his way through the State of Illinois was giving careful consideration to the politics that were bringing back old concerns to the nation builders in Washington City.

"So's I says t' him, I says, you might want to think agin' over that, Mister, I says."

The long Abe, propped himself up in bed and continued a conversation that had begun the night before. Leonard Swett, the occasional contributor to the conversation and on this particular trip Abe's traveling companion along the Illinois Eighth Judicial Court Circuit, nodded as the haze of sleep lingered in his tousled head. As an attorney and law partner of William Herndon, Abraham Lincoln continued to travel the Illinois circuit after his retirement from active politics. Still his juices had begun to be activated by the current political situation mainly in Washington City.

Lincoln had watched Senator Stephen A. Douglas, the Senator from Lincoln's own State of Illinois, promote and succeed in getting the Kansas-Nebraska bill passed in the U.S. Senate and then by a thin margin of thirteen votes passed in the House. Lincoln himself had even argued and debated against the bill at various times in several places.

"Ya see Douglas got himself made Chairman of the Committee on Territories and got the Nebraska Territory, some use to call it the Platte country cause o' the Platte River, he got that made into two territories so he could have sumthin' t' offer both the Northern boys and the Southern too. Then the Government bought the biggest share of the land of th' Indians and moved them south and west so the territories would be free fer white settlers.

"Don't forget, I went up against Douglas back in '40 when I was stumpin' for William Henry Harrison and Douglas was fer Van Buren for President. We locked horns several times. And jest 'cause Harrison won, don't mean that I bested Douglas; not by a long shot. Ya' need to watch out for 'em. He's a smart 'n."

President Pierce, decidedly pro-slavery, had eagerly signed the Kansas-Nebraska Act into law certain that Kansas would soon be another slave state.

"The feller with the newspaper said that this new bill would assure peace through majority agreement concerning the slave question when the territories got t' become States," Lincoln continued in his high, shrill voice. "But I says t' him, 'ya might be a little surprised', I says, 'it could mean a passel o' trouble nobody's a figerin' on.'"

"What could go wrong?" asked Leonard, with half hearted interest. "Let those folks decide what kind of State they want and go on about their business. Besides there are still a few Indian Reservations left. How could all this hurt?" Leonard stretched, yawned and fell face first back into his pillow.

"It's not gonna be as simple as it sounds, I'm a feared," muttered Abe, as he reached for his trousers; long-legged but still didn't quite reach his shoes.

"You're just sayin' that, on account o' Douglas says it's a sure fire cure for all the fuss over the territories," came a muffled voice from the pillows.

"'Fraid not; t' begin with, almost every one figured that Missouri Compromise of 1820 wasn't going to solve anything. Then they came along with the Compromise of 1850. That was a big joke the first minute."

"You didn't say much about it," countered Swett. "In fact I didn't hear you take a stand one way or the other."

"Wouldn't 'a done any good: it didn't please anybody, North or South, and wasn't going to. California was made a free state and the District of Columbia got slave trading banned and the bill said that the territories of New Mexico, Arizona, Nevada and Utah could be slave or free as the people there wanted. Sound familiar? Douglas didn't invent *popular sovereignty* any more than I did."

Stephen Arnold Douglas
1851

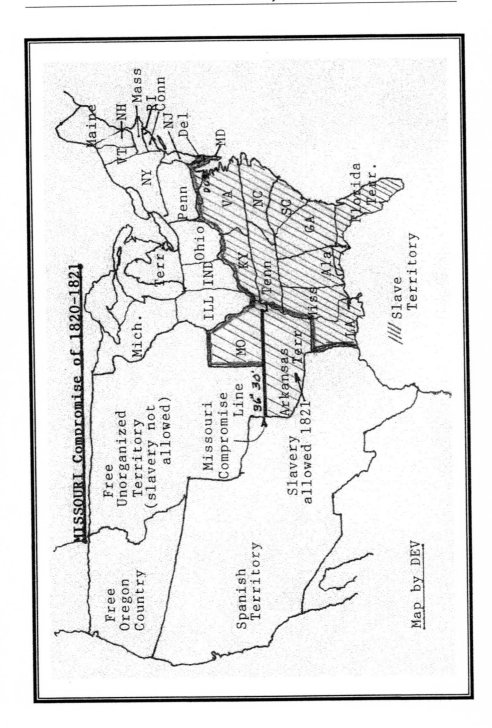

MISSOURI Compromise of 1820-1821

Maine
VT — NH — Mass
RI
NJ Conn
Del
MD
NY
Penn
VA
NC
SC
GA
Florida Terr.
Ohio
Mich. Terr.
ILL IND
KY
Tenn
Miss Ala
LA
MO
Arkansas Terr.
Free Oregon Country
Free Unorganized Territory (slavery not allowed)
Missouri Compromise Line
36° 30'
Slavery allowed 1821
Spanish Territory
//// Slave Territory
Map by DEV

"So," said Swett taking more of an interest in the conversation. "Didn't that please the South? Everyone knew since it was southern territory it would become slave."

"Not necessarily. That's where the rub came in. The North couldn't get the Wilmore Proviso passed *(which would ban slavery in territory taken from Mexico)* but the South was still afraid that the Indians and Mexicans in those Territories would balk at slavery."

"But some Indians own slaves," replied Leonard. "I've heard that the Cherokee's own slaves."

"So they do but those in the southern territories can see the tables turned on 'em by some of the whites and first thing ya' know it turns out that ya' got Mexican and Indian slaves as well as the blacks. Maybe Southern whites will have the money and power to get it done; anyway that's the thinkin' of some I've heard."

"I still say," replied Bill, "that now there will be even more places that the people will be able to make up their own minds."

"Don't know how much good it's a gonna do 'em. The Fugitive Slave Act went along with it ya know. That means that anyone can go after his property any time he wants and he can take that property just about anywhere he wants; free territory, free state or slave.

"No such thing, just you wait and see. Feller told me jest yesterday that the rumor is that a bunch of unhappy anti-slavery activists, Northern Whigs and the Know-nothings are gittin' t'gether up in Michigan and are gonna form a new political party. I already knew about that 'cause I've been in on it too. And I intend to help 'em if I can. Gonna call it th' Republican Party. They are gonna see to it that this slavery business is dealt with once and for all. That'll bust things up, wait'n see. B'sides, it shouldn't be up to just the folks that live in the territories."

"Huh? Why not? They're ones that have to put up with what happens in their own part of the country," replied Leonard.

"Ya forget," said Lincoln as he tried to tuck in his long- tailed

13

shirt. "That territory is owned by the Federal Government which means it is owned by ever'body not just those that live there. The Louisiana Purchase was paid for by all o' the people and until it is turned into States it should be handled by the will o' all the people. That's the way the law read up 'till now. And I'm a'feared that once the people realize that that's all changed there's gonna be a ruckus."

Abe Lincoln had watched, along with many people, the surge of '*movers*' as they headed west hoping for free and fertile farms in the former Indian land known as the Nebraska Territory. Now that it had been divided into two, the Kansas *and* the Nebraska Territories, the idea was to let the people that lived in each area decide for themselves whether they would have slavery or not; sounded simple.

"There wasn't supposed to be any more slavery north of the southern border of Missouri according to the Missouri Compromise and that was pretty much accepted by most everyone," continued the Illinois lawyer.

"Then all of a sudden the South realized that *all* that territory which *might* end up being free was even bigger than all the Southern States put together. That got them pretty worked up; so…now, all those folks from down south will come a rushin' in here to try to get a leg up on those comin' from the north. That's trouble in the brew pot. Be prepared. See if I'm not correct!"

Leonard Swett noted, and not for the first time, that when his friend Lincoln began to warm to his subject his "back-woods" vernacular began to disappear and his speech began to become more polished and took on an air of professionalism. Lincoln had become one of the more prominent speakers of the state and surrounding areas.

Eli Thayer's Immigrant Aid Society, in the process of being organized and financed back East by such men as Amos A. Lawrence, promised to funnel more and more interest and home seekers into the Indian lands of the central plains. It was to be a venture, claimed Thayer that would benefit the future farmers and his investors alike. Share in the wealth of the land and the fruits of those willing and eager to settle the empty fields of fertile Kansas. Empty, of course, except for the Indians that had lived in and used the lands for centuries as well as those that had been relocated from their homes in the East. These Native Americans would be perplexed by the idea of *owning* parcels of the land that was placed for their use by the Great Spirit and then when the government would explain how it was *"willing"* to pay for the land, the Easterners would educate these red men right out of their heritage.

"So," answered Leonard in a less than enthusiastic reply, "the Indians will make some money and move on. What's wrong with that? Sounds like just a business deal to me."

"It's a business deal all right. You've been a lawyer and in politics enough to catch on to his game," said Lincoln looking for a shoe that had been kicked under a small writing table. "Douglas is trying to deal himself right into a railroad line across the north part of the country. He figures if he makes it possible for the South to get another state or two across the central part of this country they will go along with allowing the trans-continental railroad to run through Illinois instead of insisting on a southern route." Abe shoved his large foot into the shoe and sat back musing to himself. "That Douglas is a shrewd one too. He knows the South isn't anxious to have a lot of commerce and smoky factories cluttering up their cotton and tobacco land and they are fairly certain they can get by with just enough railroads to get to the east coast and a few northern markets. Yes sir, that Steve Douglas is a canny feller."

"Come on, then, gentlemen of the slave states. Since there is no escaping your challenge, we accept it in the name of freedom. We will engage in competition for the virgin soil of Kansas, and God give the victory to the side which is stronger in numbers, as it is in right."

—Senator William Seward, on the passage of the
Kansas-Nebraska Act, May 1854

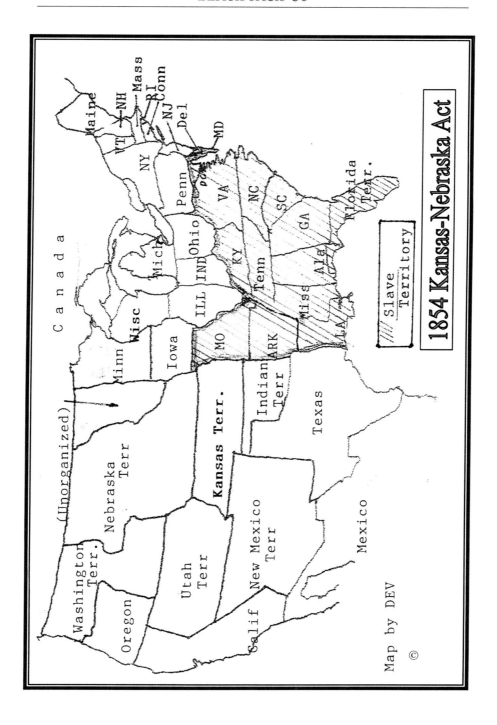

1854 Kansas-Nebraska Act

/// Slave Territory

Map by DEV ©

Chapter 3

Platt County Missouri's Senator David Rice Atchison, a large man originally from Frogtown, Kentucky; entered Transylvania College in Lexington, later read law and moved to Missouri in 1830 after being admitted to the bar. A man that had become used to a local type of success, he was elected to the Missouri House in 1834. His work on the petition to Congress for the Platte (Nebraska) Purchase endeared him to his constituents to the extent that a new Missouri county was named for him.

In 1843 the Governor named Atchison to fill the remaining time in the Senate seat of the late State Senator Linn, which made Atchison the youngest senator in Missouri history and the first from the western part of the State.

Due to excessive celebration Atchison slept through the biggest portion of his unique achievement of being President of the United States for one day. President-elect Zachary Taylor refused to be sworn in on the Sabbath which caused President Pro Tem of the Senate, D. R. Atchison, to fill the position for twenty-four hours. Although Rice was not formally sworn in, he was heard to make the statement, "You must admit; mine was the most honest administration we have ever had." If in fact he was the President, he would also be by far the youngest to hold that office.

In his Senate speech of 1853, concerning the Territory of Nebraska he said "...*I have always been of opinion that the first great error committed in the political history of this country was the Ordinance of 1787, rendering the Northwest Territory free territory. The next great error was the Missouri Compromise.*"

He could now assure his constituents that the Kansas Territory was theirs for the taking. Atchison and his close friend and author of the 1850 Fugitive Slave Act, Virginia Senator James Murray Mason, had been ecstatic at the prospects of additional slave states in the West.

In fact, when the Kansas-Nebraska Act was passed on May 30th within hours Atchison telegraphed his mostly pro-slavery constituents;

"Take the land: it's yours!"

With his prompting, Atchison's constituents in northern Missouri anxiously raced across the border into the Kansas Territory and staked out claims, then returned to their holdings in Missouri.

Even in early May, squatters were making their claims as far as two miles from Fort Leavenworth and had begun laying out a new town they would be calling *Leavenworth* to capitalize on the name of the fort. The mostly Platte County Missourians were made up of farmers looking to extend their crops. Scattered among those promptly claiming land were even some free-staters looking to take their advantage ahead of the horde of settlers they knew would soon follow.

The "Free-Staters" were sort of an off shoot of the *"Free Soil"* party formed in 1847-48 back East. They were afraid the people moving in to the new territory would be *"a bunch of squatter sovereignty"* people. Their motto was *"free soil, free speech, free labor, free men"*.

Back home in Missouri, Atchison beamed as he watched hundreds of emigrants flood Independence and St. Joseph as they prepared their journey toward the promise land of plenty. That land would become fruitful and rich on the backs of slaves from Missouri and the southeast. No reason to make the arduous and difficult journey all the way to California or Oregon. The future, the immediate future of progress and Southern Power lay just across the Missouri River.

"I spoke with Secretary of War Jefferson Davis just a few days ago and we agreed that we were well on our way to cause the dream of President Pierce, that is to calm the difficulties of this slavery question, that his dream would soon become a reality," stated Atchison to several members of his men's club in Westport. "This cloud of dissension will quickly pass as soon as the territory is settled and sends its representatives to Washington City. Gentlemen, I foresee a great future for all of us that have invested in our cause. We will not be denied our rightful credit for establishing a formidable power that can be exercised to achieve greater things in our country's capitol."

Applause and hand shaking accompanied nods of approval as David Rice Atchison raised both hands, one holding a glass of brandy and the other a large cigar, in a less than forceful effort to discourage the laurels directed at him.

"You've done it again, DR," a voice came from the group of Missouri business men that crowded around the Senator.

"No, Gentlemen, not me. I have only pursued and carried out the duties with which I have been relegated. I am only the voice and shadow of those of you who have entrusted me with your wishes and designs for the future of our great country. These accomplishments are but an echo of your voices directed to our President. And, I must humbly admit, your voice, through me, has caught his ear and been recognized as the most progressive way toward an even greater country."

"You know Senator, since the death last year of Bill King, President Pierce has been without a vice president for over a year now. We see no reason why, what with all your splendid ability you might............" Applause and cheers went up throughout the room.

"Gentlemen, gentlemen, please; I would never presume to approach the president nor have anyone even suggest such a thing to the Congress. It's true, I have been assisting and advising the President since the untimely demise of our esteemed leader Vice President King but you must remember I have sworn to devote my strength and energies to serving the great State of Missouri and that must be first and foremost...." er hurmph, " at least...ah...for the present."

The clamor of back slapping, noisy vocalization and clinking of congratulatory glasses, was being over matched by the outrage that surged through Ripon, Wisconsin, where the new "Republican Party" was being formed; a party that was certain it was on it's way to producing a President of the United States that would rectify the injustices that were being forced on the country by the South.

The South had been use to overwhelming the legislature due to the fact that they could send more representatives to Washington City than could non-slave holding states. Although the slaves could not vote they were still counted and consequently included in the population numbers that determined how many representatives went to the nation's capitol.

The new Republican Party would change all this. This was a group of dedicated men, backed by the esteemed Horace Greeley, who in an article in his *New York Tribune,* had declared that American freedom was being seriously threatened by the passage of the Kansas-Nebraska Bill. These new Republicans would negate this action by nominating a man they were certain would lead America to a fair and equitable solution to the problems of properly governing the new territories. This man they would choose was the man known as *The Pathfinder* and find a path he would; a path toward freedom and honest government for his country through this new political party.

John C. Frémont had made his mark by mapping most of the Oregon Trail and even having a mountain named for him. He had been a major in the Mexican War and was of significant help in the annexation of California becoming one of its first Senators. Frémont would assure the party he was prepared to lead again!

It was certain to be North against South; anti against pro; clouds of trouble coursing toward the now sunny skies of peace.

Franklin Pierce - 1852

Chapter 4

Wednesday May 3, 1854

"Are ya really gonna do it, Abrael?" asked Jeremy with a soulful look on his face.

"I'm sorry Jeremy, but I feel I must." He looked down at the young lad. "I'm going to miss our times together although you probably won't miss the lessons and reading assignments."

"Gee, Abrael, I really kinda' liked it. Thanks to you I can read better'n almost anyone I know."

"It's very important, Jeremy. Now you can expand your education any time you wish just by reading books about places, ideas and using your imagination. You'll grow up to be a fine man; I know it."

"But it won't be as much fun with you gone."

Just then Jeremy's father entered the room. "Jeremy can't talk you out of it can he?"

"I'm afraid not, Sir. I have actually waited longer than I intended but it isn't easy leaving…well…my family."

"And that's just what you have become, Abrael; one of the family."

"And," said Mrs. Potter as she stood behind her husband, "that's what you'll always be."

It was just as hard as Abrael thought it would be to leave but he had spoken his mind when he said he had waited longer than he planned.

At first he wasn't certain how he would make the journey to the soon to be Kansas Territory. His mind had been made up during a conversation with one of the local farmers and even Mr. Abert.

"We get most all of our stuff from St. Louis cause that's where the main railroad is and the steamers. If you're gonna' head west, I suggest that you head for St. Louis and pick your best means of transportation from there. There are lots of folks headin' that way on account of the free land they say there's gonna' be." The merchant looked up and down at Abrael. "Figure it's gonna'…well…be easier t' get along out there?"

Catching himself, he hurriedly continued, "I mean t' get yourself a place a' your own."

Abrael was use to having remarks made that were aimed at him being a Jew so he thought little of it. Right now what was on his mind was getting to his starting place.

"I guess you have a point, Mr. Carson. St. Louis would give me a lot more options. Thanks for the advice."

Mr. Carson shook his head as he watched Abrael move on down the road. "Hope he knows what he's getting' into."

"I can help load up here and then unload there if you'll just let me ride along," said Abrael. Marshall Simms had a pair of wagons heading for St. Louis loaded with boxes of personal belongings of all sorts. He had been hired by a family that had given up trying to make a living growing a vineyard and was moving back to St. Louis. Simms gladly traded Abrael the ride for free labor.

"Leavin' at first light, Tuesday morning. Can ya' be ready?"

"You bet I can," replied Abrael.

"Got much to take along?" asked Simms.

"A bag of clothes and a few books; nothing I can't carry in both hands."

"See ya' Tuesday, then."

"All right," thought Abrael, "today's Friday. That means… it struck him that in just three more days he would be leaving for… who knows what?"

"Well," said Mr. Potter, "I guess that's that. We were sorta' hopin' you'd change your mind but in a way I'm glad ya' didn't."

"Papa," exclaimed Mrs. Potter.

"Well, Mama, I just mean I'm glad he's got the gumption to strike out and give his dream a chance. It's gonna be hard work and you'll be runnin' into things you've never had to contend with before." Mr. Potter put both hands on Abrael's shoulders. "Like I say, I'm proud of you. You're gonna make it and make us glad we can call you one of our family."

Tuesday morning dawned bright and sunny and it found Abrael standing next to the wagons belonging to Mr. Simms.

"Climb aboard. The Wilson's have their things ready for us. They left yesterday afternoon. We'll get their belongings from the old house here and then we'll be on our way."

It would take the better part of two weeks to make the trip depending on weather, breakdowns and the disposition of the animals.

During the day, Abrael would visit some with Mr. Simms' driver Matthew but most of the time just ride in the back of the wagon and do a lot of walking. He tried to read but found his mind wandering and trying to imagine what he would do first when he got to St. Louis.

Mr. Potter told him to see if he could find a man by the name of Thomas Colburn or William Walker Rust. They were Mormons also and might still be in St. Louis. If so, they could be a good deal of help to Abrael. It shouldn't be too hard to find The Church of the Latter Day Saints. Maybe they could even help him locate a Synagogue. It would be nice to worship in a real Synagogue again. And maybe they could steer him in the right direction. He wasn't looking for help as such, just advice.

He had some money saved and he knew how to stretch it out although he had little idea what his expenses would be. Most people he had talked to had never ridden a train or a steamboat and hadn't heard anyone say what it would cost.

"I can work if I have to," thought Abrael. But he didn't want to experience much of a delay if he could help it. He had finally started and he wanted to keep going as quickly as possible.

"Well, this must be it," said Matthew. They were in St. Louis in front of a medium size, well kept house several blocks west of the Mississippi River. The Wilson's had left a note that Matthew found the evening before right after they had arrived with the wagons. The note told them where the Wilson's were temporarily staying and to come get them when they were ready to unload.

"You'll have to ask around," said Mr. Wilson. "I would have no idea where you'll find any Mormons. I bet if you find a policeman he can tell you."

"Good a way to start as any," thought Abrael to himself.

It was late afternoon when the wagons were unloaded and the Wilson's said Matthew and Abrael could stay in the vacant house that night if they wanted to. Matthew would start back in the morning and Abrael would look for the Mormons and a Synagogue.

In a bookstore the following day, Abrael had picked up a copy of *The Occident and American Jewish Advocate* published in Philadelphia. It was the main Jewish publication available, listing articles, sermons, reviews of various Jewish organizations and Synagogues.

The store keeper told Abrael of a Synagogue over by Fifth and Green and gave him directions.

The Rabbi was a kindly gentlemen and was pleased to visit with Abrael and talk about his plans.

"Abrael," said the Rabbi, "I am having a few friends over for a brunch this afternoon, I wonder if you would be so kind as to attend. We would love to have you and I imagine it has been some time since you have had a real kosher meal with a group of your own people. Would you come?"

Abrael hoped he didn't appear too anxious when he accepted the invitation.

"Fine, fine," exclaimed the Rabbi. "I will be ready to leave in about an hour."

"If you don't mind," replied Abrael, "I would like to just sit here in the Synagogue and wait. It will give me some peaceful time to collect my thoughts."

"I understand, my good man. It will do you good. You might say a prayer while you're waiting, and if you would, remember me as well." The Rabbi patted Abrael on his yarmulke, smiled and walked away in the dim light of the Synagogue.

That afternoon Abrael had been introduced to all the gentlemen present and had eaten the first real Jewish meal he had in years. It was a joy to be among what he felt was *his people* again; to hear the bits and pieces of Yiddish spoken and to listen to some of the conversations. These conversations were much more up to date about current events and the disturbingly unstable state of the country.

A small, yet rather stately, gentlemen in a well tailored business suit approached Abrael late in the afternoon and inquired as to Abrael's plans.

"I know you said you were headed to the new Kansas Territory but just what do you intend to do after you get there? You are much too well educated to become a mere farmer and it would seem that other opportunities would be rather rare."

"Yes Sir, you're correct. I do not intend to be a farmer. What I would really like to be is a Rabbi, but since I have neither the training nor the opportunity to get that training I have decided I would be the next best thing, a teacher."

"Ah; a teacher."

"I know that sooner or later there will be a great need for teachers and while I will probably have to start out with just a small and possibly even primitive school, I can fill a need and soon there will have to be better schools and maybe even small colleges… someday."

"It's a noble ambition, and not a surprising one from such a noble young man." Reaching out his hand, the man said, "My name is Abeles; Simon Abeles. I have a clothing and dry goods establishment here in St. Louis. I have a friend that has approached me about a business deal in the new territory."

Mr. Abeles went on to tell of how his friend had considered starting a similar business next to Fort Leavenworth. Through Leavenworth passed many travelers heading for places everywhere from just a few miles into Kansas, to Utah or all the way to Oregon. He was certain that as soon as more Indian land was made available the traffic would increase to the point that the demand for goods would far surpass that available under the present circumstances.

"From what I hear," replied Abrael. "I wouldn't be surprised if he were correct."

"This will happen sometime in the fall, you understand," continued Mr. Abeles, "but I believe I have made up my mind to make a small investment and join my friend in his venture."

"Well, I certainly hope it works well for you, Sir," said Abrael.

"But, just a minute Abrael. May I call you Abrael?"

"Of course, Sir," said Abrael.

"What I have in mind is including you in our idea."

"I appreciate your offer, Sir, but I would have no money to invest. Besides, as I said, I'm interested in teaching, not being a merchant." Hurriedly, Abrael added, "Not that it would not be an honorable profession and do a great service to…"

"Hold on, my anxious young friend," said Mr. Abeles with a

chuckle. "What I had in mind was that you could oversee the shipment of goods I will be sending and perhaps assist in getting the establishment in proper shape to begin business. While you are doing that, you can take stock of your new surroundings and decide from more first hand knowledge exactly how you want to go about getting yourself set up in your own situation."

"Oh," said Abrael, a little embarrassed. "I guess maybe I could do that. But you said this wouldn't get started until this fall. I can't very well wait around...I mean...I haven't any..."

"Ah, not to worry," said Mr. Abeles. "If you would consider a rather menial position for the present time, I could use some help in my store here in St. Louis. You will be earning a small wage while learning about the business. I have an idea you have a good head on your shoulders for business as well as education."

"Oh well," said Abrael, "I would appreciate the opportunity and I assure you I would do my best to learn all I could. I'm told I am a good worker and I will apply myself in every way I can although depending upon the job, my wardrobe may not be suitable."

"Fine; then It's settled. And don't worry about your attire. Remember I have a dry goods store. Now have you a place to stay?"

"Not really, Mr. Abeles, but I'm certain I can find a place that will do for a few months."

"Nonsense my boy; we have a carriage house behind our home that has a loft above it. It can be made suitable I'm sure."

"But I wouldn't want..."

"I won't hear another word." Turning to the others Mr. Abeles said, "Gentlemen, I would like you to meet my new employee and future representative to the new Kansas Territory, Mr. Abrael Kepper."

The months seemed to fly by. Abrael worked at Mr. Abele's store, learning all he could, making amazing progress, according to

Mr. Abeles. The stone warehouse in Fort Leavenworth was ready and the goods here in St. Louis were packed and crated.

"We'll be corresponding regularly Abrael and I'm certain you will find your niche in the new land. Remember, if you decide to stay with the business, I'm convinced you could be a real asset to the company. You learn quickly and do your job well."

"Thank you Mr. Abeles, I'll keep your offer in mind," replied Abrael, hoping he would not have to take advantage of it; yet it was something he could fall back on if necessary.

After wandering back and forth on what seemed like miles of wharfs, dodging carts, crates, bales and large men with even larger burdens, Abrael located the shipping office of the *Sonora*; a side-wheel wooden hull packet. It was 220 ft long with a 32 ft beam, at 363 tons with three huge boilers. The captains were Joseph LaBarge and William Terrill. It was first launched in St. Louis in 1851 and regularly steamed the Missouri and sometimes the Red River. Abrael was just double checking on the arrangements that had already been made since the shipping date was the following day.

Aft of the *Sonora,* Abrael paused to watch men unloading the *Arabia*, a smaller, 181 ft long side-wheeler that had just returned from up river. It was just a year old and still sparkled like new. Abrael wondered if he could get any useful information from some of the crew but they were not obliged to talk while the Captain was watching from the near railing.

Never mind; it was done. One more day and Abrael was headed for Kansas.

Chapter 5

Fall, 1854, Leavenworth, Kansas Territory

Abrael had been exceptionally busy for several weeks, doing almost everything. He was unloading, opening boxes, stocking shelves, checking inventory, sweeping, dusting, making price signs, creating displays, occasionally making a sale and compiling a list of items of all nature that needed to be ordered.

His immediate supervisor was a man named Levi Meyer. Levi was sort of an assistant manager and Abrael was his *"do everything"* assistant. Abrael didn't mind being delegated all the chores and more menial duties. It left him free to observe all the workings of the company and even get away by making an occasional delivery. It was during the deliveries that Abrael was able to learn just what was going on; and there was a lot going on.

In March the Otoe and Missouri Indians ceded their lands to the Government and by May so had the Delawares, Shawnees, the Iowas, Kickapoos, Kaskaskias Weas, Sac and Fox and a number of others. Some had held back certain areas for a reservation, the size depending upon the tribe. Then came the passage of the Kansas-Nebraska Act.

Weeks prior to the passage, people from Missouri had crossed the border and much to the displeasure of the Indians, had staked out the better plots of land. Even in June the *Squatters Claim Association* was formed, by mostly Missourians, at a trading post just west of Fort Leavenworth at Salt Creek Valley.

Their charter began…*"Whereas, we the citizens of Kansas Territory <u>and other citizens of the adjoining State of Missouri</u>……"* This was actually an agreement among squatters and not a legal or binding statute.

Word had been received that organizations in New England were raising money and forming groups of "settlers" to populate the new territory.

One of the first was the "New England Emigrant Aid Society" to which the Massachusetts Legislature had granted a charter of incorporation on May 4, 1854. With capital of over four million dollars, President Eli Thayer began selling stock in the Boston company to outfit groups of settlers to be sent to the new territory. Many other companies of similar nature would soon be formed in both the North and the South; each with its own agenda which would be aimed at populating the Territory with people of their particular political persuasion; free or slave.

The successful plotting of the town of Leavenworth in May had allowed interest to quicken. The building began immediately and by September Leavenworth's first newspaper, *The Herald,* was in business located in the very first building in town. Then, of course the Rees warehouse was built at Main and Delaware close to where Keller was building the *Leavenworth House*; a rather rapidly built hotel of some questionable stability.

"Gee, I had no idea Leavenworth was growing as fast as it is," said Abrael to Levi as they sat drinking a cup of hot coffee toward the end of the afternoon. "Then when the crew on the steamer said we would be docking first at Kansas, I didn't understand what they meant."

"Kansas," said Levi, as he wrapped his hands around his warm cup, "is what they use to call West Port. Y'see it was Westport Landing at West Port Missouri. Then three or four years ago a bunch of investors calling themselves the Kansas Town Company incorporated the town and called it Kansas. So now Westport Landing is at the town of Kansas. They first spelled it 'C-a-n-s-e-z'. Not sure why, but there it is."

"It certainly is a busy place. And now we're getting almost as busy."

"It'll get even busier soon too. The Murphy and Scruggs saw mill has made it unnecessary to ship in good lumber so no one has to wait for their building materials."

"I understand," said Abrael, "that they were the first saw mill within miles."

"They were the first saw mill in the entire territory as well as building the first building around here. The mouth of Three-Mills Creek is the perfect place for a mill and they recognized it the first time they saw it."

Saturday, October 7th, 1854 was a big day for Leavenworth. It was the day the *Leavenworth House* was having its formal opening. Everyone knew that the newly appointed Territorial Governor Andrew Horatio Reeder would be arriving any day now and Uncle George Keller and his son-in-law A. T. Kyle wanted to be ready.

Governor Reeder, although appointed by President Pierce was a little less than totally pro-slavery. The new Territorial Attorney General, army General A, J. Isacks, who accompanied the Governor on the steamer *Polar Star* up the Missouri River was definitely pro-slavery but kept it to himself. Consequently, at the moment, neither man was all that popular among the Missourians. It was a good thing they by-passed Weston.

Dr. Charles Leib met and welcomed them with a speech at Captain Hunt's headquarters. The new Governor acknowledged the welcome with a few words then everyone retired to a less formal and more festive evening.

Arriving on the 10th was the two United States Territorial Judges, Honorable's Johnson and Elmore from Ohio and Alabama respectively. Completing the ruling biotic community would be

Chief Justice Honorable S. D. Lecompte, who would arrive several days later.

Samuel Dexter LeCompte had been born in 1814 in Maryland, was educated there and in Pennsylvania where he graduated with honors. He came to Missouri and helped form a group of pro-slavery men that intended to establish a town in the Kansas Territory that would hopefully become the capital of Kansas Choosing some Wyandot Indian land along the Kansas River in what would become Douglas County they made their claim.

SAMUEL DEXTER LeCOMPTE
The only know photograph of Judge LeCompte. Courtesy Kansas State Historical Society

The town of Bald Eagle, founded in July of 1854 by these men, one of whom was the grandson of Daniel Boone, was renamed Lecompton, in honor of the Chief Justice, and would become a pro-slavery center of Kansas along with the town of Atchison. Both towns had been founded this very year just in time for the political contest that was about to determine the fate of the new Territory.

"Did you see that crowd down around the hotel?" asked Abrael after Levi finally arrived late that morning.

"That is why I'm late. I stopped to inquire and I fear the trouble is just beginning."

"In what way" asked Abrael? "You look worried."

"Governor Reeder just announced he is going to make a trip through the Territory and visit with as many of the permanent residents as he can find to see what the general opinion is toward a free state as apposed to a slave state."

"But I thought that is what his job was," replied Abrael. He pulled a crate toward him and began to pry away the top boards. "Isn't he supposed to find out what the people want?"

"Yes, but that worries the hell, a…pardon, out of the Platte County Self-defensive Association."

"Who are they?"

"They are the self appointed Missouri overseers of the new territory. They expected to be the top advisers, or probably dictators I should say, to the new Governor."

"Now what happens?" asked Abrael, freeing the last board.

"There's going to have to be an election to choose the representative that will be sent to Washington. And that person or persons will report the wishes of the majority of the voters."

"I see what you mean about trouble."

"I believe these people know what they want and should have an opportunity to have it," said Governor Reeder to his Attorney General Isacks. "After two weeks of traveling around talking to various groups in small towns, churches and even cabins, I'm convinced that most of these people are level headed folks that just want a peaceful place to live and raise their families. They want no part of angry politics."

"I found the same to be true during my trip south," replied

General Isacks. He had traveled as far south as Fort Scott and, as did Governor Reeder, spoke with many people interested in a permanent future in the Territory. "I'm really impressed with the land," he said. "It is going to make a very good agricultural addition to the …government, some day." Governor Reeder noticed, without comment, General Isacks' avoidance of the term 'Union'. He was well aware of the General's leanings toward slavery but by unspoken arrangement, they avoided direct mention of the subject. General Isacks did not, however, avoid contributing overtures in that direction to his new acquaintances from Missouri.

KANSAS TERRITORY

FIRST TERRITORIAL APPOINTMENTS
JUNE 29, 1854

GOVERNOR – Andrew H. Reeder – Replaced by
Wilson Shannon September 1855
SECRETARY – Daniel Woodson

UNITED STATES MARSHALL – Israel B. Donaldson

CHIEF JUSTICE – Samuel D. Lecompte

ASSOCIATE JUSTICES – Saunders N. Johnson
Rush Elmore

ATTORNEY – Andrew J. Isack

SURVEYOR GENERAL – John Calhoun

TERRITORIAL TREASURER – Thomas J. B. Cramer

CONGRESSIONAL DELEGATE – (later elected)
J. W. Whitfield

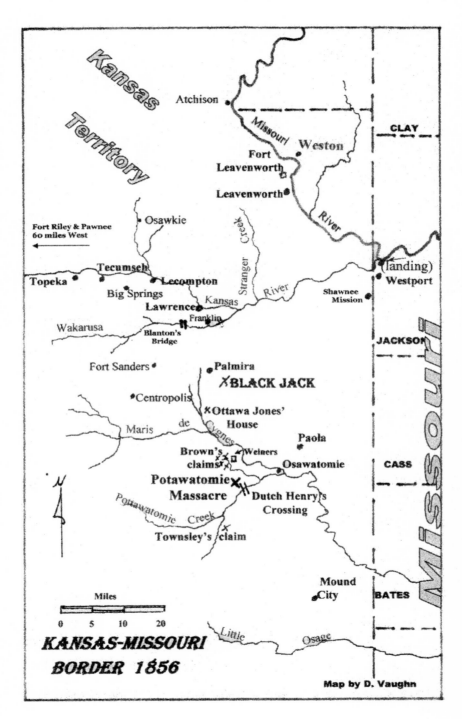

KANSAS-MISSOURI
BORDER 1856

Map by D. Vaughn

Chapter 6

Friday, November 10, 1854.

A notice was printed by *The Herald* and posted through out the Territory stating that Governor Reeder had divided the Territory into sixteen Electoral Districts and after a week or so added one more so that a Territory wide election for Congressional Delegate could be held on November 29th. The Governor thought it was much too soon to attempt to elect a Territorial Legislature. He was certain the authentic Kansas settlers wouldn't have a chance.

In Missouri reaction was swift. The Blue Lodge headed by David R. Atchison and the Platte County Association group immediately scheduled a meeting in Platte City to plan their action.

"Why should you let a group of fanatics and demagogues a thousand miles away determine what the land around you is going to be like?" raved Atchison. "They have no interest except making money to line their own pockets. When you live as close as we do to the Territory, what ever happens there is going to greatly affect our future. Consequently we have a perfectly good right to have a say in the outcome of that election; and by god that's exactly what I intend for us to do. We're all going to get involved in this. And that goes for every County in the western part of the State if necessary." Cheers went up throughout the crowd along with shouts of approval.

"Just tell us what to do and you can count on us," they cried loudly.

"I'll tell ya," boomed Atchison's voice. "We're gonna send thousands of voters to the election and make sure we get the representation we deserve. And I'd rather see the whole territory in the bottom of hell than a Free State!" Drinks were waved in the air as a bond of determination cemented the crowd in one purpose.

After some discussion it was decided that General J. W. Whitfield would be their nominee for the position of Territorial Delegate. It was also decided to wait to see just what stand Governor Reeder would take before exerting pressure from the Missouri side. The Governor had brought with him the Honorable Robert P. Flenneken, a Pennsylvania man who was somewhat a Free-Stater but was considered manageable by Reeder and Pierce.

With the help of Claiborne Jackson and Samuel Young, prospective *voters* were assigned districts and instructed to vote and then block the doors to keep the local rabble away from the polls.

"Everyone knows," stated Atchison, "that the only people they are sending out here from the East are nuthin' but the dregs and scum of society they want to get rid of. They wouldn't know anything about voting properly anyway!"

"Guess everyone is getting ready for the election," said Abrael. "You going to vote Levi?"

"Oh yes," stated Levi firmly. "They aren't gonna scare me away."

"I don't believe I'm eligible since I don't own a home here or any property. Besides I don't understand all this political talk I hear from the customers. Some of them get really riled up."

"You bet they do, Abrael, and so should you. You are as eligible to vote as anyone and it's your duty to do so. Besides the law is written so loosely that practically all you have to do is just be there to vote. But you better be ready for trouble!

"If you want this land to be free you must take your stand just like the rest of us."

"Of course I want the land to be free. That's why I came here but I thought I had to have a claim or something."

"No such thing. You've heard that the Platte County bunch is coming, haven't you? They want to be sure the Delaware Trust land stays under their control while the Free-Staters are fightin' for the same thing."

"Yeah," asked Abrael, "what is that?"

"It's the land the Government got from the Delaware Tribe earlier this year and has opened for settlement. That Platte County group is a pretty fierce organization and there are more just like 'em. There's the Blue Lodge, that's the one Atchison belongs to; and there's the Sons of the South, the Social Band and they are fighters. The Platte Association constitution states that all free blacks are to be removed from the territory; they don't want slaves to be able to hire themselves out for money and you being white can't associate with a black under any circumstances.

"Why every stranger that came into Weston was questioned and if they said they were even considering being a Free-Stater they were told to leave town or else. One couple had even started a house and when it was learned they were abolitionists they were threatened with whipping if they didn't leave within twenty-four hours."

"Golly, what happened to them?"

"They left! But they went on to Kansas. They weren't going to be intimidated enough to go back east. There are lots of stories like that and that is the way it will be if the Missourians get control of the new Territory too.

"The paper last week said that Atchison was getting together five thousand to head for Kansas on Election Day. You think that doesn't spell trouble?"

George Haggis, a frequent customer and prominent figure in Leavenworth, overheard part of the conversation between Levi and Abrael. "If you don't mind my interrupting, Gentlemen, I would ask if you read the letter Governor Reeder sent to a group of those professing to be concerned Kansans."

"I guess not," replied Abrael.

"It might provide you with a different opinion of the new Governor. There was a meeting here in Leavenworth a couple of weeks ago; one which I attended, that was composed of supposedly concerned Kansas Citizens. From the beginning I noticed there weren't that many men I recognized from our own city. Then when I saw the meeting was being led by John Doughearty, I knew most were from Missouri. Doughearty is very big around Clay County.

"They presented a letter that was closer to a demand, to Governor Reeder, that included a number of complaints about his neglect to consider the wishes of these "Concerned Kansans".

In short order he replied that he could see through their gesture and he was not about to be coerced into ignoring the true wishes of the people of Kansas. He stated that;

> *"We shall always be glad to see our neighbors across the river as friends and visitors among us, and will endeavor to treat them with kindness and hospitality. We shall be still more pleased if they will abandon their present homes and dot our beautiful country with residences to contribute to our wealth and progress, but until they do the latter we must respectfully but determinedly decline to allow them any participation in regulating our affairs."*

"He went on to say…'if you don't mind we'd rather you stay out of our way and let us do our job as we prefer."

"I guess that does make a difference," replied Levi.

"Yeah, but it won't make him very popular with Pierce," said Abrael. "Still I'm glad that apparently I can vote along with everyone else."

"You bet you can, young man," said Mr. Haggais. "It's your duty!"

All afternoon of Tuesday the 28th of November, north of Fort Leavenworth at Rialto Ferry, crowds of Missourians loaded with tents, on horseback, in wagons and even on foot clambered up the bank of the Missouri River and struck out for their assigned voting place. A few would have to travel most of the night but determined they were. In all probability only the settlers within half a days ride would be aware of what was really happening, know anything about the three candidates or much care.

Since the majority of the voters, it turned out, would be pro-slavers it was certain that General J. W. Whitfield would be the Delegate.

Originally from Tennessee, where he served in both houses of the State Legislature, the General had shown his self fearless during the Mexican War, after which he was appointed Indian Agent for the wild Kansas Territory.

His opponents were Robert P. Flenneken, approved of by the Governor as a fair and honest man and backed by Pomeroy and Robinson[1] of the NEEAC for strictly commercial reasons; hoping for development of Eastern businesses in the Territory.

Also on the ticket was John A. Wakefield who professed to be the only truly Kansas territory resident running and an honest to goodness Free Stater.

The morning of the 29th the polls opened at the Leavenworth Hotel. Things were relatively quiet for most of the day. George Keller bustled around the Judges and touted his new establishment to the people from Missouri. If anyone indicated they had leanings toward the Free-State side of the ballot they were hassled and given a hard time. A number of people approaching the voting window would change their minds after taking a look at some of those rough sorts hanging around. Although there were those, such as Abrael and Levi, who made it clear, they were not to be intimidated. A couple of anti-Semitic comments were made but ignored by both men.

"Notice how welcome we Jews are?" said Abrael.

"We add variety," replied Levi.

Most of the voters from across the river voted early and many left to get back to their homes and work now that they had done their duty for God and Atchison.

---

1   Charles Robinson, to become first Governor of the State of Kansas

After supper the liquor began to flow more freely and an occasional fight broke out. Again a few Kansas Free-Staters who had farther to travel arrived near closing time and were badgered about their choice of candidates even though by that time it was pretty clear that General Whitfield had the office of Delegate in his pocket.

"It wasn't as bad as I thought it would be," said Abrael to Levi as they walked back to the store where Abrael was living. "After listening to you talk about the election I figured it would be a hand full of trouble."

"Well," said Levi, "that is just the beginning. Wait until they try to get a Territorial government set up. Then we'll see how smoothly it goes."

Still, Abrael had cast his first vote. He was proud of that. It was his first really free and independent act as a man. He was his own man now in a free land in which he could build his own home and future. It felt good!

COURTESY KANSAS STATE HISTORICAL SOCIETY

Chapter 7

Friday, December 1, 1855

Most of the reports were in and it was clear that General Whitfield was the new Congressional Delegate from the Kansas Territory. There had been many stories, most of them true, that elections were 'fixed' due to outsiders coming into the precincts and voting. Only in Lawrence and one other smaller precinct had the Free-Staters won, and by quite a favorable margin. Yet it was not enough to sway the entire election.

Now it would be Governor Reeder's job to get started on the spring election of the Territorial Legislature. He was certain that by that time there would be enough Free-Staters in Kansas to off-set the pro-slavery group if that was truly the way they wanted the Territory to go and prepare the way for Kansas to enter the Union as a Free State. He had already been accused of putting off the election for just that reason even though it was not his real intention. As he watched the new emigrants enter the Territory looking for farms on which to establish politically free homes it was quite evident that the tide would certainly turn toward the often heard "free land, free men, free State".

Abrael was getting anxious about his future. He had a good job and place to stay and yet it wasn't what he had come west for. *The job* was just a means of making a living and his *place to stay* was not a "home".

Abrael had given some thought to the town of Topeka that was being formed by some free thinking business men, intent on making the town one of commerce and business. The streets were being laid out wide and in perfect squares. When someone asked why the main street was so wide, the answer came that it would help provide a fire break in case some of the frame buildings would catch ablaze. The perpetual Kansas wind would easily carry embers for dozens of yards and as yet only one stone building was planned. Not being certain just what he would do there he decided to put off any definite plans

Earlier in the fall Abrael had made a trip to Liberty, Missouri to inquire about a teaching position at the new William Jewell College. It was a private college founded in 1849 with a grant from Dr. William Jewell of Columbia, Missouri. In addition was the Liberty Ladies College located there, but Abrael thought it would be foolish to apply and didn't relish the thought of teaching only girls.

Upon arrival at William Jewell College, Abrael made his inquiries and was directed to the office of a Mrs. Jordan.

"May I help you?" inquired the young girl behind the desk in one of the outer offices.

"Yes, thank you," replied Abrael, nervously fumbling with his hat. "I am here to apply for a teaching position."

The young girl smiled at this handsome young man that stood in front of her. "I'd be more than glad to help," she said, looking over the top of her gold rimmed glasses. "If you could....."

At that moment several people entered the office, apparently with some sort of situation that required immediate attention. There was a confusion of voices as Abrael tried to tell the young girl his name. She scribbled on her small piece of paper and at the same time tried to acknowledge the apparent demands being placed on her by the others for immediate action.

"Just a minute," she said to Abrael, "I'll be right back. Amelia, would you watch the desk?" Another dark haired girl nodded and took her place in the straight backed chair watching the group of people hurriedly leave to resolve their problem elsewhere.

Abrael took a seat against the wall next to the door. He looked around the room and occasionally at the new girl. She seemed busy with some papers and a very large, black bound book. "History," she said quickly as she saw Abrael watching her. Abrael smiled but the girl was back reading before she could notice.

Abrael had arrived around mid morning and it was now mid afternoon. He had watched as several girls came in, occupied the chair behind the desk, then left. The girl he had seen when he first arrived never did return.

"I wonder," said Abrael finally running out of patience, "If I am going to be able to speak to the person I'm supposed to see about a teaching position?"

"I wondered why you were sitting there," said the latest girl, rather wide eyed. "Does she know you're here? Does she have your name?"

"I have no idea," replied Abrael, trying hard to keep a civil tone. "I believe it was someone named Jordan. The girl earlier wrote down my name, at least I think she did."

"I'll see," said the young lady. She removed her glasses and disappeared into another office. In a moment Abrael heard another door open and close, then open and close again.

"Mrs. Jordan is just about to leave but she will see you for a moment."

"Oh, that's just fine," thought Abrael.

"You're a man!" exclaimed Mrs. Jordan as she finally looked up. Abrael had entered and stood waiting several minutes to be acknowledged.

"Yes, Ma'am."

"But it says here that you are Amy Pepper."

"I don't know how that happened Ma'am, but the name is Abrael Kepper."

"I see. You're J...not from around here."

"No Ma'am." It didn't take long for Abrael to understand the implication.

"You must be from back East, perhaps St. Louis. I understand you have people in that area."

"No, Ma'am," said Abrael. He fully understood her meaning about the large St. Louis Jewish community but he refused to play that game. "My parents died a number of years ago so now I have no people left. I'm originally from Rhode Island and I did live in St. Louis for several years but I now reside in Leavenworth; Kansas Territory." He was pretty certain that wouldn't give him any advantage but he was quickly becoming irritated.

"I'm afraid, Mr. Kyper…"

"That's Kepper, Ma'am."

"Ah, yes, Mr. Kepper. I'm afraid we have no positions open at the moment."

"I see," replied Abrael. "Well I was in town on business and thought I would drop in and leave my name and instructions as to how you might reach me. Should you have a position, you may notify me and I'll be glad to consider it. I cannot, of course, make any promises, but I will give it some thought. Good afternoon."

Abrael bowed very slightly, turned and left the room, the building and the town.

"I'm a lucky man. I didn't get the job," said Abrael out loud.

Chapter 8

February, 1855

"Oh… I don't really know," replied Abrael to Levi's question. "It's just that I don't feel like I'm getting anywhere."

"But you have a good job, a good place to stay and who knows you might even become a partner someday."

"I don't want to seem ungrateful but I don't want to be a partner and I don't want to live here in Leavenworth the rest of my life."

"Do you really know what you want, Abrael?" asked Levi.

"Well…I think I do. I know that someday I want to teach…"

"So…you can teach here; right here in Leavenworth. Have you tried? I bet you could get a job right here. And you know this area. We're already established and growing fast."

"I know, Levi, but I doubt I could teach here the way I want to. The people here have very biased ideas and if I can't have the freedom to teach what I think is right I won't teach at all."

"So you know what is right? You know just how to make all the right decisions?"

"You must know what I mean, Levi. Of course I don't know everything, but I know what real history teaches us and that is just as important as ciphering, spelling or any other subject. And we both know around here they aren't going to let teachers tell both sides of a political question especially.

"Besides, I want to find a place and build my own home."

"So now you're a carpenter, Mr. Teacher?"

"Com' on, you know what I mean. I want to have a place of my own so maybe someday I can raise a family and all that."

"And I supposed you have a girl all picked out, already?" said Levi with a smile.

"Oh sure; I've had lots of time to pick out a girl. No, I want to get settled first. You know, since Kansas became a Territory they have been dividing the land up into counties and more towns are sprouting up than you can shake a stick at.

"There's Shawnee County with Topeka and Tecumseh; there's Douglas County with Lawrence and Palmyra; there's Franklin County with Centropolis; and Lykins County with Paola and Osawatomie."

"Ohhh-sa what?" asked Levi with a grin on his face. "Who ever heard of such a name?"

"I was told that it is a combination of two Indian tribes; the Pottawatomie and the Osage. The town has been there awhile."

"Just where did you get all this information about towns and such?"

"I've been talking to the freight haulers and the stage coach drivers. They've been all over that part of the country."

"That's all south of here isn't it", questioned Levi?

"Yeah, I guess it is. Topeka and Tecumseh are a ways west."

"So that where you're going?"

"Dunno yet," mused Abrael. "But I gotta do something. I can't just sit here."

"March 30, 1855, is going to go down as the day the world was created around here," stated Levi as he put down a copy of the *Herald*. "Governor Reeder says that's the day we're going to have the election for the Territorial Legislature."

"Do you really think there is going to be that much trouble?" asked Abrael in a worried tone.

"You bet I do."

"Me too," said George Hay, one of the customers standing around the warm stove that stood on the center of the room. "You should have heard what Atchison said to his bunch at their meeting. He said that they were sending hundreds of his guys over and that they wont be takin' *no* for an answer at the poles. He said that this was their land to take care of and by god that is just what he was a' gonna do no matter how many people got in the way of their guns and bowies."

"Surely they wouldn't kill people just to keep them from voting," said Abrael.

"Don't count on it," replied Levi. "You know what they have done to some of the Free-Staters so far."

"Yeah,' said another by-stander, "I read where Stringfellow wrote to his Southern friends in Congress that they had gotten Whitfield elected and they would get their people in the Territorial Legislature the same way, and for them not to be concerned one bit. He said there will be no *April fools*" from Kansas in Washington City, just 39 more men that think like Missourians."

"Well, Reeder has taken a census so he knows how many eligible voters there are. That'll give him more control over this election," said Abrael.

"And just who is going to back him up? The army won't do anything and Atchison and Stringfellow are already trying to get President to replace Reeder."

"And they'll get it done too. Just watch and see," affirmed another in the crowd.

"I hope you're all wrong," thought Abrael. To him it was getting scary.

Chapter 9

Friday, March 30, 1855

Abrael and Levi were ready to get an early start to the voting place but was interrupted by a shipment of cloth and miscellaneous items just in on an early boat from St. Louis.

"Guess we'll have to take care of this first," said Abrael rather disgustedly. "I wanted to get over there and back before they had time to get any ruckus started."

"You still think there will be trouble?" asked Levi, as he moved some boxes out of the walk way.

"I'm as certain as anything. I can just feel it in my bones. There is real trouble in the air."

Mr. Saunders, an early arrival at the store was looking over a stack of starched, white Sunday shirts. "We saw the steamboat *"New Lucy"* bring a load from Missouri in yesterday. They were a rough lookin' bunch, I can tell you. Every one of them had a piece of rope in a button hole, around their collar or waist. And some of them carried a length of rope around their shoulder. That was their way of intimidating other voters and letting people know just who they were."

"And I saw bowie knives and pistols in a lot of belts, too," offered another customer as they began to gather around.

"You might be right Abrael," said Levi. "Let's get going, now!"

As they approached the hotel where the voting was to take place there were already a large group around the window that had been temporarily remodeled to accept the voters' ballots.

"And just who do you think you are?" asked one of a pair of rough looking characters apparently guarding the ballot box in the window.

The elderly man who had approached the window replied, "I'm a farmer from just west of here, if it's any of yer biness."

"Just how do I know that you're a legal resident of the Territory, old man?"

"How do ya know I ain't? I'll sign yer paper if'n that's whut it takes, but elsewise git out'n my way."

"Yeah, com'on, let 'em vote so's the rest of us kin git a chance," hollered someone from further toward the back of the line.

"Who's the loud mouth back there?" hollered the ruffian at the window. "You want trouble c'mon up here!"

"Now old man, either show me sumthin' that proves you are a rightful voter or git!" With that the ruffian shoved the elderly man out of line and started to turn away. Just then a large hand landed on the bully's shoulder. The crack of the collarbone could he heard ten feet away.

The ruffian screamed as he grabbed at his shoulder.

"You lay a hand on my father again and it'll be a neck bone that cracks." The voice came from a broad shouldered man that stood near six feet, four with dark brown hair almost down to his shoulders.

The area around the window cleared and the elderly man placed his folded ballot in the box and turned without even looking up at his son. The son and two other men likewise dropped in their ballots and walked away together toward a large wagon parked in the street.

The ruffian, clearly a Missourian, had been helped inside the hotel and given a stiff drink of whiskey.

Quiet reigned for the next ten or fifteen minutes until another rough looking character with a piece of hemp hanging from the button hole in the collar of his jacket walked from the hotel into the yard and stood next to the window.

Abrael and Levi watched him as he looked from one voter to the next.

"Lemme see that," he growled to a smallish man about to push his ballot into the box.

"You've no right to look at my vote," protested the little man.

"Shut up, you."

"Hey, Carl; you ever see this here fella before?"

"I ain't never seed 'im 'round town none," replied the man who was apparently Carl. "Y'all from hyear 'bouts?" The question was directed to the small man still clutching his ballot with both hands.

"'Y'all'?" whispered Abrael to Levi. "Does that sound to you like *that fella* is from around here?"

"You can bet he is one of them that came in yesterday on the boat and who knows where he came from before that," replied Levi. "You were right about the trouble. Let's see if we can't get our vote cast and get back to the store."

After several other voters had managed to vote, Abrael and Levi reached the window.

"Name?" asked the man next to the ballot box.

"What difference does it make what my name is?" asked Abrael as he reached to drop in his ballot.

"Oh; you're one of them!" growled the man with a sarcastic grin on his unshaven face.

"And that is supposed to mean…?" said Abrael as he grabbed the man's wrist and pulled it away from the slot in the top of the box. Abrael's ballot dropped in as he released the man and remained at one side of the window. He was just waiting for the man to try to keep Levi from placing his ballot in the box.

"It means that you ain't one of us and we don't need your kind here in our country", sneered the man as he rubbed his hand.

"You're right; we're not one of your kind," replied Abrael. "Because 'our country' will be free from bullies like you and we will be able to do as we damn-well please."

Raising a fist, the man blurted out, "Why you Jew…".

The words barely left the man's mouth when Abrael had grabbed both of the man's lapels and stomped down hard on the man's left instep. Then Abrael's right fist split the man's left cheek and the man went down.

When the dust cleared Abrael and Levi had been pulled from the crowd and men from both the voting line and those from inside the hotel had finally restored order.

"Do you know that you just attacked a judge who was appointed to guard the voting place?" asked a heavy-set man wearing a suit and string tie.

"He's not th' judge," shouted a man from the voting line. "Tom Marsh was supposed t' be the judge and they wouldn't let 'im in this morning."

"That will be sorted out later," replied the man in the suit. "If there is any more difficulty caused by you trouble-makers, I'll see that the Sheriff is called and possibly even the troops from the fort."

"That is one side of you I never thought I would see, Abrael," said Levi as they made their way up the street toward the store. "I didn't think teachers were fighters."

"If you are a Jewish kid growing up back east and you leave your own neighborhood, you better be able to fight. Still, it was a stupid thing to do," replied Abrael rubbing the skinned knuckle of his hand. "I once read that the first man to raise a fist is the first man out of rational ideas."

"Then you have nothing to worry about," said Levi, with a big grin. "He started to swing at you first."

It's not funny," said Abrael as he looked at Levi and started to snicker and then began to laugh and shake his head. "Let's keep this to ourselves," said Abrael.

"Fat chance of that; the story will probably beat us back to the store."

And it practically did. That and many other similar stories concerning fights, people turned away from the voting place and voters obviously from out of the Territory were repeated all weekend. Monday morning, folks that had remained in town we eager to tell their stories and hear those of others that had made the trip to town to vote.

"We had some relation come up Saturday from Lawrence and they said it was really bad there. Colonel Young and even Claiborne Jackson brought in hundreds of people. They had wagons full of men, men on horseback and they even brought a couple of canons; but they were for show I guess. They didn't fire 'em off.

"There were some fights though and a lot people turned away so they couldn't vote. Finally a bunch of Free-Staters got together in a big group late Friday, guns and all and marched to the poles and got their vote in; for all the good it did, they were so out numbered."

"That's okay," said one customer reassuredly, "Reeder wont let them get away with it again, I bet."

"But what can he do?"

"He'll figure out somethin'."

And so he did. The same voting experience was seen throughout the entire Territory. Missourians had crossed the border by the hundreds bringing their threats with them. When the results were in, it was evident to everyone how the ballot boxes had been stuffed. When asked if they had their claims staked and intended to stay, one roughly dressed, bearded Missourian replied, "None o' yer damn business whut I do!" They had been told "you can vote even if you only been here an hour".

More than twice the number of people indicated by the recent census cast a vote on March 30th. Most Missourians refused to take the oath of residence and shoved their ballot in the box over the protests of the judges. Some pro-slavers even brought their own printed ballots and used them.

Dr. Charles Robinson and a group from Lawrence met with the Governor and pleaded with him to declare the entire election fraudulent, but to no avail. This caused Robinson to contact Eli Thayer and describe the troubling times and the great difficulties he envisioned. Robinson begged for weapons such as the new Sharps rifles and sent G. W. Deitzler east to get them.

Governor Reeder was at a loss as to how to handle the situation. Finally he took the most blatantly false results and scheduled new elections for the 22nd of May. It was a futile gesture but he had to do something.

Chapter 10

The Free-State squatter had to be dealt with and soon! At a meeting on April 30th of the "Delaware Squatters", held in Leavenworth, the rules and procedures for handling the matter had been hotly discussed.

"I probably shouldn't a' gone but I did," said old man Rogers. He was one of the original Leavenworth residents and was greatly disturbed at what was happening to "his" town.

"I goes down to Cherokee and Levee, ya know, down where there's that big old elm; well they was shouting and shakin' their fists and swearin' that the land was ther'n and no body was gonna git none of it. Well Sir, there was this one feller, name a Cole McCrea, I seen him around some, well he got right upset with Malcolm Clark who was headin' up this here meetin'. Clark told him a time 'er two to shut up 'cause he weren't involved but it didn't do no good.

"I guess at some point, I couldn't hear all of it, but anyway that there old Scotsman, McCrea got up in Clark's face and the fust thin' I know Clark's got a bullet in 'em and McCrae is headin' fer the river. Probably would'a been hung if'n it hadn't been fer Pitcher and some other fella. They got him in a wagon and took 'em off to Fort Leavenworth."

A Free-State lawyer by the name of William Phillips had also attended the meeting and, at this meeting just as in the past, heartily agreed with the few who were protesting the one-sided rules of obtaining land. They immediately claimed he was the man who had slipped the pistol to McCrae. That same evening he was found guilty and ordered to leave the Territory by the afternoon of the following Wednesday.

When the committee assigned to keep track of Phillips found that he had disobeyed the order he was kidnapped and taken to a

Weston warehouse, stripped of his shirt, had half his head shaved, was tarred, feathered and taken to the middle of town on a rail. There they had an old Negro slave auction him off. He was finally released and allowed to return to Leavenworth. Stubbornly he still refused to leave Leavenworth and was shortly thereafter hanged by members of the Delaware committee. No action was taken against the perpetrators.

> *"...hell, we had thousands of people over there at that election and most of 'em are going to stay there. We can control every acre of prairie and timber and bring in thousands of families with their slaves. We'll have slavery all the way to the Pacific Ocean!"*
>
> David Rice Atchison, Missouri

"That does it! I'll not stay in such a place as this," said Abrael. "I'm not certain where I will go but hopefully it will be where people can be safe with their own beliefs."

"Just where will you go, young man?' asked an older man that had been listening to the conversation between Abrael and some other customers.

"I don't know yet," replied Abrael. "There are towns springing up all over the eastern part of the Territory. There must be someplace I can find a little peace."

"In this day and age, my young friend, peace must not only be sought after but paid for by effort and determination."

"I've heard that all my life," said Abrael in an exasperated tone. "Is there fighting and disagreement everywhere? Where are the people that just want to get along and...."

"Hold on; getting upset won't get you what you want." The older man spoke in a slow, quiet voice.

"There can be peace when peaceful people congregate and not

allow that peace to be disrupted. It will come only when a firm stand is exhibited and it is made known that interference will not be tolerated. That takes courage and determination. When we are willing to stand up to the trouble makers and make them understand that the penalty for disruption will outweigh their gain, then my young friend there will be peace. Bullies pick on the weak and those not willing to stand up to them."

"You speak as though you have been through all this, Mr........ ah Mr..........."

"I'm Dr. Wood,[2] from Lawrence. And yes we have been through this and I must admit I doubt it is over."

"So things are no better there then they are here," replied Abrael, with a somber tone in his voice.

"Perhaps not; but we are much closer. We have made a beginning, a good beginning, and we will continue to try and to build and someday we will have our community become a place of peace and freedom."

"I've heard you folks are getting ready for big trouble over there," spoke one of the men listening to the conversation. "I hear they are building a big brick building that's gonna be used as a fortress and their getting' ready for the Missourians."

"It's true," replied Dr. Wood. "What we are building, with the help of the Emigrant Aid Society, is a hotel; the Eldridge Hotel. And it will be constructed so it might help stave off an aggravated attack but that is only a very minor appointment of the design. Our desire is for a peaceful co-existence. Even though we are strongly against the importation of slaves into our Territory, we have no desire to alter the way the Missourians live as long as they keep it on their side of the border."

As Dr. Wood spoke, he watched Abrael. He could tell the young

2   Dr. Wood would become the physician for the 1st & 2nd Kansas Colored Infantry to be formed in 1862 by James Lane.

man was frustrated but he could also see determination in his bright eyes.

"It will be worth it to you to join us and work with us. You will find your peace. You will find it by earning it and becoming a part of the effort to bring it about."

"Another challenge," thought Abrael. But the man was right. He had learned that most things are worth only what one must pay for them. And if done right, this could become a good thing, a worthwhile thing; the thing Abrael was searching for.

"Think they could use a teacher?" asked Abrael.

Chapter 11

Monday, March 26, 1855

Along with Abrael Kepper, fate had chosen another young Jewish man to head for the new Kansas Territory and ultimately take his place in the work of forming a new and hopefully free land.

August Bondi stood on the deck of the river steamer *"Polar Star"* gliding up the Missouri River headed for Kansas Territory. *"Go West, young man..."* Horace Greeley has said in *"The New York Tribune"*. August had just read the article and that very same day purchased a pair of saddle bags and was now on his way.

August Bondi was a twenty-two year old Jewish boy, late of St. Louis, before that, from a time in Texas and recently back from visiting his parents in Louisville, Kentucky. August might have stayed in Kentucky had he found suitable work but perhaps there was still more adventure deep in his nature that was begging to be turned loose.

Whatever the cause, today he was standing next to his new friend Stephen Withington, from Massachusetts. Stephen also was heading for...well, where ever the boat went. Without even a change of clothes; armed with a rifle wrapped in a blanket he was as anxious as his new friend August to see just what was around the bend. August would soon learn that his friend would not have the determination and staying power that was borne deep in the nature of the young Bondi boy. Before long they would part company but for now it was a shared adventure.

After several bends in the river and the trails, the pair arrived at Lawrence, Kansas Territory on Wednesday April 4 of 1855.

One might say that the settlement of Lawrence had been started by a few Missouri Border Ruffians who had staked some claims in the tall grass and sunflowers and returned to their permanent homes in Missouri. Members of a group sponsored by the New England Immigrant Society and lead by Dr. Charles Robinson had also chosen almost the exact same spot near Mount Oread to settle.

As it turned out, several Missourians had remained and challenged the new comers to the right of ownership. When subtly confronted by small arms, the Border Ruffians headed back east after deciding they would let their more influential friends in Missouri attend to the legal details.

"Whut you gonna tell 'em when they find out you let them Yankees run us off'n that there claim?" said one of the scruffy men from across the border.

"Me? I didn't see you pullin' no iron on 'em."

"I ain't in charge o' nuthin. It ain't my claim t' git shot over. Anyways I heard 'em talkin' and that tall older fella said he don't shoot less'n he's fixin' t' bring sumptin down and I believe 'em."

The community, after being called New Boston, Wakarusa (being near the small river of that name) and several other things, was finally named Lawrence after the prominate Bostonian Amos A. Lawrence.

By this time a number of groups from the north east had arrived and settled not only in Lawrence but Topeka, Osawatomie and a number of other small villages determined to become free-state communities; and most of which had encountered similar difficulties with absentee "claim owners".

Bondi and Stephen stayed in Lawrence for a few days and then headed further south. Finding a spot to suit them they began to build a small shelter for themselves.

"This isn't turnin' out like I thought it was gonna," said Stephen one evening after a day struggling to strengthen their "cottage".

"You can't get anything around here even if you can afford to buy it," replied August. "There's no lumber, no nails and hardly any staple goods t' live on."

"I don't know, what do you think?"

"You thinking of leaving even after all the work we've done?" asked August. He could tell Stephen was ready to move once more, searching for who knows what.

"I just don't see that we're gonna get anywhere. Didn't you say that your old boss Benjamin was thinking about coming out here?"

"That was when I was In St. Louis. I don't know if he is still of the same mind."

Jacob Benjamin agreed that he was still of the same mind when August Bondi approached him about the move after arriving in St. Louis close to a month later. Together they purchased the needed tools, a horse apiece and started back west toward the Pottawatomie, in Kansas Territory.

"I thought this was supposed to be free country," said Benjamin, as they proceeded south. A number of the settlers they had met owned slaves and would be quick to inquire as to the politics of the two newcomers. Free country indeed it was but there were a goodly number from Missouri that would bring their slaves just across the border but still be close enough to run back in case of big trouble.

"My friend here," August would say, "came from Germany not long ago. Me I'm fresh from Texas. Lots of pretty girls in Texas, but I'm not much on ranching."

With Benjamin's accent as prominent as it was, the story was accepted by most, especially since the pair was moving on.

They traded their horses for a wagon and two yoke of oxen believing they could better manage their new claims with the wagon for hauling and the oxen for plowing. That was, when they learned how to plow.

"Mein name ist Herr Eberhardt. Ich kam von Wurtemberg in Deutchland."

"Ah so," exclaimed Benjamin.

Their next new found friend was Dr. Eberhardt. He had been in the Territory for a couple of years and explained that his horses had died during the winter and he would help the boys find good claims in exchange for the loan of the team so he could plow.

They quickly agreed and after selecting a claim for each of them went to work improving those claims with a "cottage" for each of them. From that time on they were friends. Being able to speak in German gave them a sort of kin-ship and came in handy when others were around and they wanted to keep their conversation private.

"Du kannst den Buschstaben an lassen Dutch Henry's," Eberhardt told August when he enquired about sending a letter to his friends in St. Louis.

"Dutch Henry" Sherman along with his brothers "Dutch Bill" and James had a sort of "trading post" type enterprise they operated at Pottawatomie Crossing on the California Trail. Even though the cigar box used as the post office could boast of never having lost a letter, the same could not be said for cattle belonging in the surrounding herds.

Night time seemed the normal time for cattle to disappear from the local herds, especially the Indian herds. After a little branding work cattle would quickly be sold to the government buyers and traveling cattlemen heading north or south.

A large man, mostly disagreeable, Dutch Henry would always inquire about a visitor's politics. He would make it known, with out a doubt that he was pro-slavery and he was going to do his part to see that the Kansas Territory would end up the same way. He also advised that since August was another one of the Jew bunch building up around the area that being anti-slavery would just add to the problems he might look forward to! In time Abrael too would have to deal with Dutch Henry and his philosophy; but now he was interested in learning more about the growing town of Lawrence.

****

There was a little more to Lawrence than Abrael imagined. He arrived in town early that morning and slowly made his way to Dr. Wood's home taking note of the homes and business' that were under construction.

"We founded our Free State Society in January of this year," Dr. Wood told Abrael. "We elected our officers the first of February, in March had a meeting of the Union School District and picked a site for a school. And, I am proud to say, we have collected enough money for the material. They say it will be closed in by the first part of May."

"That's wonderful. It looks like you folks don't let the grass grow under your feet."

"Ah, there is so much to do. And we still must keep watch over our shoulders. We are constantly being harassed and threatened. Still, we have mail going to and from Kansas City, Osawatomie and Fort Scott.

We are fortunate to have the first anti-slavery newspaper in the Territory, *The Kansas Tribune*. It is published by John Speer who came here from Ohio; been in the newspaper business all his life. He tried having his paper published in Kansas City, but when the publisher learned it was an anti-slavery paper, well...he cancelled the contract immediately. John even tried to set up in Leavenworth but had the same difficulty. So, being determined, as I said, he came to Lawrence; and we are grateful he did.

"We also have a barber and... oh well, you aren't interested in all of that."

"Oh yes I am," replied Abrael. "Of course I am mainly interested in teaching. What do I have to do?"

"Well according to what we are being told, they are writing the Territorial school laws now and they should be published by sometime in August. They say each teacher must have a certificate and be passed on by three trustees and one inspector. They must be of high moral character and know their subject."

"But I have no actual certificate. I began teaching some of the local children when I was in Missouri. Not in a regular school but in their homes or at the home of the folks I was living with."

"Hm; I see."

"I was fortunate to get a good education when I lived in Rhode Island. I went to school and also learned much at our Synagogue. I was only fifteen, but they said that I learned very fast for my age and I am willing to study any subject it is felt I am deficient in...ah... I mean *in which it is felt I am deficient.*"

Dr. Wood laughed. "I see you have knowledge of English grammar that might be a little more than what would be required by the standards around here."

"But Sir; there will be young people leaving here to go east to college and it will be required there."

"A point well made, young man. I believe between us and some friends of mine we will be able to find you a position. However I cannot say just how soon that will be. You may want to find other work to sustain yourself for the near future."

"Thank you, Sir. I believe I can do that. I also want to see about making a home for myself."

Chapter 12

May, 1855

One sunny afternoon, August Bondi happened to notice a couple dozen unfamiliar cattle grazing close to his not yet completed cabin. They seemed unconcerned that they were moving along his claim which caused August to wonder if he had some new neighbors.

"Sorry 'bout the cattle," said the young man on horseback as he and another young man rode toward August. "We'll try to keep 'em closer t' home."

"Don't give it another thought," replied August as he removed his hat and wiped his forehead. "We only have two pair of oxen so there's plenty of prairie to go around.

"You fellas new here? My name is August; August Bondi. Got a partner just next door name of Jacob Benjamin."

"Brown's our name," said the first rider. "I'm Jason and that's m' brother Owen. There's two more of us back at our claim. We just got here not long ago ourselves. May have some other kin folk joining us soon, too."

"That's fine; glad to meet you". August smiled and nodded.

"And if you're wonder 'n," said Jason, "we're Free-Staters! Got no use for slavery a'tall; not here or anywhere. You been hounded any by that bunch from Missouri?"

"Oh, some I guess. There was this one man who said he was a preacher. He said his name was Barnaby. He also looked around and said he thought my claim and Jacob's was owned by some Missouri friends of his and we better look for some place else. So far no one's shown up to throw us off so I'm not too worried. "

The two Browns had dismounted, shook hands with August and let their horses graze a bit.

"I did meet that Dutch Henry fella," offered August. "He seems none too friendly; not to us any way. Doesn't seem to care much for Jews and certainly doesn't like our politics.

"Also ran into a fella by the name of Wilkinson. Said he was a pro-slaver and even been elected to the new legislature last March. Guess he won't be neighborin' much.

"We don't care for slavery either," said August, leaning against the unfinished cabin. "If you know anything about us Jews, you know we've been looking for a place to live and let live for a long time.

"My friend and I just came from St. Louis a few months ago hoping to get a fresh start here in the Territory. Maybe even start up a trading business. We have some friends in St. Louis, the Wiener brothers. They are going to help us get our little business started, I think."

"Good for you," said Owen. "If you and your friend have any trouble you just come a'runnin'. We'll be ready to give ya' a hand and we got th' weapons t' back it up!"

August waved as the two Brown boys began to drive their cattle back to their claims. It was more than a little comforting to finally find someone who was on the same side of the fence as he and Jacob.

Friday June 1, 1855

"Glad you're back," August said to Jacob and Dr. Eberhardt who had returned with the siding to finish the two cabins.

"Trouble?" asked Jacob.

"Nothing yet, but could be down the road." August told Jacob about recent events and the people he had met.

"Well, we didn't expect to be welcomed with open arms but I'm glad the Browns are at least close. Maybe nothing will come of all this since the elections are over and folks can get back to making a living."

"Hope you're right," said August. "I'm anxious to finish up here and get to back to St. Louis. The sooner we get our goods together the sooner we can begin bringing things back here and get started on the store."

Monday June 25, 1855

"I guess you may go along Abrael, but you must be responsible for your own provisions and what ever equipment you feel you might need." Dr. Wood, having been elected Council Member from the Third District, and several other townspeople were preparing to go west to Pawnee, just outside Fort Riley for the first meeting of the First Territorial Legislature.

It was hot and travel would be very uncomfortable. A two story stone building had been erected to house the legislature while in session, a log cabin had been built for the use of the Governor, and accommodations had been made for the Legislators at the Fort and at several boarding houses in Pawnee.

"Don't worry Doctor, I'll manage quite well and I must see what will happen when you and the others try to be seated."

"Don't be looking for trouble Abrael. I am quite certain that it will at least be orderly if not pleasant."

When the party arrived at Pawnee it was evident that all concerned had come prepared to stay in the immediate vicinity of the stone building in which the meetings were to be held instead of at the Fort. Wagons, cook fires, and tents were everywhere.

Prominent among the on-lookers was a man who was to become well known to Kansans and Missourians alike; a man who would soon be called the Grim Chieftain, James Lane[3]. Lane had come to the Territory to try to form a western arm of the Democratic Party.

---

3   James Lane would become Senator Lane of Kansas and form the first black regiment to fight in uniform in the Civil War. See *"The Chance"* also by Dale E. Vaughn.

He had tried rallies in Lawrence and the surrounding area with very little success. Now here he was at Pawnee making certain everyone knew he was here and just who he was. He was determined to insert himself in the very center of the politics of the day. If he did not fit their mold he would fashion one for himself and cause it to become a force of great import.

Lane had studied law in Indiana and was admitted to the bar in 1840. He fought in the Mexican-American War for two years as a colonel in charge of an Indiana regiment. He served in the legislature, was Lieutenant Governor and while in Congress voted for the Kansas-Nebraska Act. Although leaning towards his Democratic background he would cast his lot with the Free-Staters.

Governor Reeder opened the session with a plea for unity and cooperation, which immediately seem to leave the room along with the hot humid air through the wide open windows on to the prairie.

The first act of the Legislature was to seat every man elected to a seat in the House and Council in the first election held in March of 1854; totally ignoring those elected in May.

The second order of business was to elect John H. Stringfellow, of the Eleventh District, as Speaker.

The Speaker's first order of business was to adjourn the meeting with an order to reconvene in the Shawnee Manual Labor School at the Methodist Mission next to the Kansas-Missouri border on Monday July 16th, of this same year; the comfort of the proximity to the Missouri homeland seemed appropriate.

Chapter 13

"The permanent character and high authority of a State constitution and the fact of its submission to a direct vote of the people of the Territory indicate that event as a signal occasion for the decision of that peculiar question. In the meantime, however, a Territorial Legislature may undoubtedly act upon the question to a limited and partial extent, and may temporarily prohibit, tolerate or regulate slavery in the Territory, and in an absolute or modified form, with all the force and effect of any other legislative act, binding until repealed by the same powers that enact it."

First Territorial Legislature
Shawnee Mission, Kansas Territory
July 16, 1855

"Can they do this, Doctor?" asked Abrael. "Can they just write in what ever they wish and ignore the wishes of the people?"

"I'm afraid, Abrael, they can claim they are carrying out the wishes of those who elected them. It is said that the Governor had a gun placed to his head, whether this is just a figure of speech or actually happened is a matter of question, but his hands seem to be tied. If he vetoes a bill they simply over ride it and it becomes law."

"The legislature says that the Governor did not have the power to overturn the first election so those of us that were elected in the May election have no legal standing and cannot be seated. They say the Judges confirmed the various elections and the Secretary of the Territory validated the election and that's that!"

"Then," put in Dr. Robinson, "the Governor declared that any laws passed at the Shawnee Mission were not valid because the Legislature did not have the option to establish the meeting place; only the Governor had that power and he did not choose to have the seat of the government moved to Shawnee Mission.

"Then why have a governor at all?" said Abrael disgustingly. "Has he no recourse?"

"He is planning a trip to Washington City to appeal to the President but I doubt, knowing the President's politics, that the Governor will have much chance.

"I was told that the Governor even felt the need to attend the first session armed with a pistol in his belt."

"I intend to write to Amos Lawrence and see if he can exert any influence on the President. Pierce is a relative of Amos' but I doubt it will do any good. Pierce thinks that the potential difficulties are just trumped up rumors being spread by the abolitionists. He won't listen to anyone but Rice and his cronies."

"Yes," said Dr. Wood. "It is easier for him that way."

"It still isn't fair," said Abrael. "I guess I am getting cynical but it seems that the government is getting more that way every day. Just look what they have and are doing to the Indians. The eastern American culture has been pushing and actually stealing the lands that rightfully belong to the Indians and has for centuries. Even President Jackson turned on the very Indians that helped him win the battle at New Orleans and took their land and sent them west to places in which no one could eke out a living."

"And now," inserted Dr. Wood, "We are doing it again, eh Abrael?"

"Exactly! Of course I know the argument. The Indians are savages. They are barbaric and uncivilized."

"What they mean," said Dr. Robinson "is they are not like us."

"What they are saying," corrected Dr. Wood, "is that we want their land and we are strong enough to push them off of it."

"And if they don't give it up we will kill them off and take it anyway," finished Abrael.

There was silence in the room for several minutes.

"I fear this is just the beginning," stated Dr. Wood in a somber tone. "There will be more violence before this is settled. I pray we can keep it to a minimum."

The Legislature continued its business; defining county boundaries, setting up school districts, establishing courts, and most of all forming a Territorial Militia. Teeth were being given the Territorial Government. They would be able to enforce the laws that would gain them their pro-slavery territory.

Saturday, July 28, 1855

"I'm afraid there is more sand in the gears of the so-called Territorial Government," declared Abrael. He had just returned from a shopping trip into town and had joined a crowd at the newspaper office.

"What has happened?" asked Dr. Wood.

"The Legislature has written to President Pierce declaring all this business about the location of the seat of the government is causing the Legislature a drastic delay in their work. They say that if the Governor is correct in his argument of where they are to legally meet, then he had no right to convene at Pawnee."

"How do they arrive at that conclusion?" begged Dr. Wood, who had come down stairs just in time to hear Abrael begin his tale.

"They say that Governor Reeder called a meeting at Leavenworth right after he arrived and conducted some official business, thus making Leavenworth the legal seat of the Government and he never changed it."

"But here's the key to the whole thing and what will ultimately bring this to a head. The Legislature wrote a letter to Territorial Secretary Woodson requesting Governor Reeder's objections set aside; Woodson immediately turned it over to Chief Justice Lecompte who agreed with the Legislature and wrote a ruling to that effect, a copy of which is in the pocket of Andrew MacDonald and on it's way to Washington City along with the complaint of the Legislature."

"Goodbye Governor Reeder," said Dr. Robinson. "Hello Black Laws."

"Exactly," agreed Dr. Wood.

Wednesday, August 1, 1855

Reeder To Be Replaced As Governor
Woodson to be Acting Governor

Washington City newspaper

President Pierce maintains that Kansas Territory has given him more worries than all of the other problems of running the Nation combined.

Reeder agreed to step down with the consideration of another appointment yet to be disclosed by the President. Territorial Secretary Woodson will be acting Governor until such time as a permanent Territorial Governor is appointed.

Andrew Horatio Reeder
Oct. 7, 1854 - Apr. 17, 1855;
June 23 - Aug. 16, 1855

Wilson Shannon
Sept. 7, 1855 - June 24, 1856;
July 7 - Aug. 18, 1856

John White Geary
Sept. 9, 1856 - Mar. 12, 1857

Robert Walker
May 27 - Nov. 16, 1857

James Denver
May 12 - July 3, 1858
July 30 - Oct. 10, 1858

Samuel Medary
Dec. 18, 1858 - Aug. 1, 1859;
Sept. 15, 1859 - Apr. 15, 1860;
June 16 - Sept 16, 1860;
Nov. 26 - Dec.17, 1860

Governors of the Territory of Kansas Appointed by the Presidents of The United States Pierce and Buchanan
(Both of Southern persuasion)
1854 – 1860

Daniel Woodson
Apr. 17 - June 23, 1855;
Aug. 16 - Sept. 7, 1855;
June 24 - July 7, 1856;
Aug. 18 - Sept. 9, 1856

Frederick Perry Stanton
Apr. 15 - May 27, 1857;
Nov. 16 - Dec. 21, 1857

James Denver
December 21, 1857 - May 12, 1858

(FOR WHOM THE CITY
OF DENVER COLORADO
WAS NAMED.)
1 SEE BELOW

Hugh Sleight Walsh
July 3 - 30, 1858;
Oct. 10 - Dec. 18, 1858;
Aug. 1 - Sept. 15, 1859;
Apr. 15 - June 16, 1860

George Monroe Beebe
Sept. 11 - Nov. 26, 1860;
Dec. 17, 1860 - Feb. 9, 1861

Acting Governors of the
Territory of Kansas
1855 – 1861
(Either between appointed Governors or if
the regular Governor had to be out of the
Territory, these men would fill in.)

COURTESY KANSAS STATE HISTORICAL SOCIETY

1 (Gov. Denver was the only acting <u>and</u> appointed Governor of Kansas)

Chapter 14

Meeting after meeting was held in and around Lawrence. Early in July the members of the Free-Staters that were elected but denied their seats in the Territorial Legislature met to try to decide what action to take.

Dr. Wood, Robinson and many others spoke declaring their intensions not to let the Pro-Slavery Legislature deter their efforts to make the Territory free.

The only thing accomplished and agreed upon was that another meeting should be held on August 14th with at least one member of each district present.

In Late July James Lane tried again to interest the people of Lawrence in forming a Democratic Party.

"I'm afraid he didn't get very far," reported Dr. Wood, who had attended out of curiosity. "I believe many people are too familiar with the Missouri brand of the Democratic Party to be interested in having one here. I must admit that Lane does have some good ideas and even more fire. He knows how to make things happen and I bet he will."

At the August 14th meeting the March election was again denounced and the pledge for freedom in the Territory was reaffirmed. This group called for a meeting at Big Springs on Wednesday, September 5th to determine the ideas and inclusions for a future Free-State Constitution. All districts should be represented so a framework could be considered.

The Following day, August 15th, more people arrived in Lawrence and another meeting was held which included the Territorial Free State Executive Committee as well as many other interested citizens and District Representatives.

Included in both groups were Cyrus Holliday, G. W. Brown

of the *Herald of Freedom*, Charles Robinson, Abrael, Dr. Wood, John Brown Jr., and Col. James Lane just to name a few of those determined to cause freedom to rule the plains of Kansas.

On Wednesday, September 5th, 1855 Representatives from every town and district had arrived at Big Springs, Kansas Territory, by every means of transportation available to voice their preference for a Free Territory. "We will not be made white slaves by the pro-slavery Missourians."

"Dr. Wood," said Abrael. "Have you heard about that Mr... or maybe Reverend Butler, I don't really know which, but he's from up on Stranger Creek; has a farm there. They say when he was on his way back to Illinois to get his family and he was ganged up on when he was in Atchison.

"He wasn't shy about letting them know he was a Free-Stater and so they called him all kinds of names and finally set him afloat out on the Missouri River on a couple of logs tied together. They even put up a flag that read '*Greeley to the rescue I have a nigger*' to let people know he was against slavery."

"I too heard the story, Abrael. They even painted an 'R' on his forehead proclaiming him a rogue. And like a good Christian he said he forgave them if he drowned. He just may be a bigger man than I."

People had been gathering in cabins, small towns, along roads and village stores to discuss and plan the kind of State they would soon have. It would be of their design without the influence and dictations from either other eastern states or even from Washington City. They had been promised 'popular sovereignty' and "*By God they were gonna' git it one way or tuther!*"

Everyone would have a chance to say their piece and input was acknowledged and listened to regardless of whether the person was a Whig, Democrat, No-nothing or independent of any stripe. The

Pardee Butler
"If I drown, I forgive you.

"Greeley to the rescue I got a nigger."
"Rev. Mr. Butler agent for the Underground Railroad"

Courtesy Kansas Historical Society

platform would be constructed so as to allow as many freedoms as practical with the number one priority to be the total absence of slavery in any form.

However; negroes would also be barred from the State, whether free or not and those owners from other States would not be interfered with when reclaiming their slaves from the State. There were many not in favor of this but it was felt that a constitution thus constructed would be more acceptable and more apt to be passed in Washington City. Enforcement of a few of the rules might be something else a little later on. It did, however, grant the right to vote to any Indian that exhibited the conversion to the white man's way of living.

One of the most important actions performed was to nominate by acclamation former Governor Reeder as the delegate from the free-state Territory.

The date for the formation of the constitution was set for the 19th of September at Topeka. Election Day would be October 9th.

"A Democrat and a lawyer; what more could you ask for," remarked John Brown Jr. to his brother Jason. It was August, the ground was hard and dry, it was too hot and now this. The new Territorial Governor Wilson Shannon would be another hand-picked tool of President Pierce.

"I thought someone said he was from Ohio," said Jason.

"He was, originally; even served one term as their Governor. I can't tell ya' why he's so Southern in his thinking, but he is a pet of Pierce."

John Brown Jr. had written his father about the turmoil in the Territory and warned him that trouble was bound to rear its ugly head soon. He had related how the area was overrun with predators, stealing, threatening and now and again even killing. "They are armed to the teeth," he told his father. And every one of them backed by some slave owner or pusher not only from Missouri but all over the South.

"There is no organization whatsoever among the free staters." he had written. And only a few of the people were decently armed and wouldn't know how to act alone anyway. They would be wiped out in no time.

"There's going to be serious trouble. I have been in meetings and heard how too many believe that all we must do is declare ourselves and write up a constitution; that will solve our problems."

"It isn't going to happen that way," he told his father. He reminded John Sr. that he had considered coming to Kansas Territory and now was the time he would be needed the most. Leaders were needed and they must remember how our fore-fathers had to prepare. "We will need arms and much ammunition. I fear a civil war is eminent!"

Chapter 15

October, 1855

Brownsville had competition. Weinersville had sprung up around the new store. The building was built and already a few goods had been put in place. To the displeasure of the Henrys' the store was beginning to be a popular meeting place and was doing a very good business.

It was not that Weiner's was taking away business from the Henry's; theirs was not the same type of business. It was that the Free-Staters were successful. Even the Indians were coming in occasionally. When the remainder of the merchandise arrived there would be even more activity.

Abrael had helped put up the building and would be a clerk of sorts for a time at least. He still had his eye on moving to Lawrence but that could wait for a time. Along with August, Abrael, Fox, Jacob, and Ash, they had enough to sell, to stock and even make a few deliveries.

August had been down sick with a bad fever and had to be treated by a traveling doctor. The fever finally broke but it left August very weak and unable to do much. Abrael stayed with him some and the Brown boys came often bringing milk and making certain there was water and bread.

Abrael had met John Brown Sr. along with the rest of the six boys and Brown's son-in-law Henry Thompson on the way to vote. John Jr. was to be the delegate from their district which covered Franklin and Anderson Counties. Abrael was impressed by the piercing blue eyes of the senior Brown. The look of determination on the man's face insured that there was no doubt as to his purpose and his ability to carry out that purpose. He stated very clearly and concisely that he was there to help stop the invasion of slavery into the Kansas

Territory. A number of years ago he had stood up in church and dedicated his life to the eradication of the slavery and he would continue until either he was successful or dead.

Everyone was looking forward to the end of October when the Constitutional Convention would be held in Topeka. Abrael had permission to attend with Brown Jr. and was anxious to see the town of Topeka.

He had been told that a two story stone building had been built on the west side of the main street in Topeka. Rumors had it that it was also being used to hide runaway slaves, store weapons and ammunition as well as a meeting place for religious and political organizations. It was said that people would heat lead and mold bullets in the basement of the building. Who knows about rumors?

But this is where the constitution would be drawn up. Here, history would be made and Abrael wanted to see as much of it as he could. Former Governor Reeder had been sent to Washington City as the Free-State Delegate but it was a lost cause. He had been dismissed by the President and could hardly expect to be recognized as an official from the Territory.

In addition Reeder's reputation was being held in question due to the facts about his real estate holdings being discovered. Reeder held land lots in at least fifteen different towns in the new Territory. It was wondered how much political pull had been used earlier to obtain these properties.

Free State Party leaders Dr. Charles Robinson and James Lane of Lawrence herded the delegates into the building on Tuesday, October 23rd. As only delegates were allowed to witness and participate in the proceedings Abrael had to remain outside watching and hoping to hear bits of conversations of people claiming to know what was happening.

One man who claimed he had taken water into the delegates said, "They can't decide what to do about the free blacks that are already here."

"I heard that there was gonna be a thousand man militia come the first of the year," said another. "My cousin sweeps and empties the spittoons and he knows for a fact."

Day after tedious day delegates would move in and out of the dark stone building arguing and waving their arms. When anyone came close enough to hear they either swore at them and told them to "get the hell away" or ran back into the building.

Abrael spent part of his time looking around the town. There were several dozen cabins and a number of commercial buildings in various stages of completion. Topeka was gearing itself to become one of the major towns in the Territory. There was even talk about making it the capitol when the Territory became a state even though most everyone knew it would probably be Lawrence.

It was learned, not surprisingly, that much of the constitution was based on the Constitution of the United States. There would be three branches, Legislative, Judicial and Executive; two houses, Senate and House.......Articles insuring freedoms, that is if you are white and a male, worship, owning property and on and on.

For twenty days the delegates studied and debated until finally on Sunday, November 11th it was announced that the constitution was complete and the voting by the citizens of the Territory would be on December 15th.

It passed, it went to Washington, it failed.

No matter! It was to be tried again and then again if necessary. The Territory would be a State and it would be free!

"There's no damn way those sons-__-_____ are going to get away with that!"

John Stringfellow spoke through clenched teeth to Wilson Shannon, Governor and President of the newly formed "Law and

Order Party". "The only constitution that Territory will have will be one we draw up and get passed. We're counting on you, now."

"John," spoke the Governor quietly, "don't get all excited. The Topeka Constitution didn't pass did it? Well don't worry; we can quote the Territorial Laws to them and see to it that anything they come up with, if it doesn't measure up to what we originally agreed upon, well it will never get out of Washington. We can claim it is treason and we can make it stick."

Chapter 16

Friday, November 16, 1855

"Good afternoon, looking for something in particular?" asked Abrael.

"Oh!" The man looked Abrael up and down, and then muttered, "Never mind; if I see something I want I'll let you know."

Abrael had seen it before and recognized it right away; that attitude toward Jews. "Well, what did he expect, a Chinaman?"

"Don't let it bother you, Abrael" replied Jacob. "He probably expected you to be German."

"Live around here Mr….ah…"

"Coleman, Frank Coleman; come from up north of Palmyra."

"I didn't think I had seen you in here before, Mr. Coleman. How's things up north? I'm Jacob."

"*Things,* as you call 'em was fine until the Free-Staters moved in. There's a bunch of claim jumpers for ya'."

"I'm sorry……?"

"They'll be the ones to be sorry if they don't stay off my property; wait and see. I don't stand for no sass or stealin'."

"A…yes Sir. Well if you see something I can help you with just let me know."

"If I see something worth the price I will. Dutch Henry said I had to watch out or I'd git took. Thought I'd just check for m'self. From the looks of things I figure he's right."

With that the sour faced Frank Coleman left the store, climbed into his wagon and headed north. Any of the new-comers to the territory would find Coleman a difficult man to deal with. He was set in his ways and was not about to bend to any changes in his world.

Charles Dow, one of the many new-comers to the Territory,

walked up to a cabin close to his newly established claim and knocked. He was hoping to get some information about his new surroundings.

"Jacob Branson's the name. What'd you say yours is?" asked the man who answered his knock.

"Dow, Charles Dow; I'm originally from Ohio."

"Really? Me and my wife are from up at Wyandotte, but from Indiana before that."

"Glad to meet ya. I filed on the claim just south of you. What happened there? Looks like a fire. Has there been trouble?"

"Guess no one knows for sure. There was a cabin there until a couple of days ago. Then in the morning it was gone."

"Anybody hurt?" asked Charles.

"Naw; nobody's been livin' there for a long time. Guess it's yours now. Got a family?"

"Nope, just me."

Dow was asked inside and offered a cup of coffee.

After a conversation that finally led to politics Jacob made the following offer to Charles. "Tell ya what. Maybe you ought to stay here with us until you get a cabin put up. Maybe I can even give ya' a hand with it."

"I'd hate to put you out," replied Charles, "I could sleep in a little lean-to for awhile."

"Not safe. You stay with us. It won't take long."

After dinner that evening the two men sat around the fire while Mrs. Branson cleaned up the pots and dishes.

"Yep," said Jacob, "been a plasterer for twelve years; learned from my Pappy. That's what I'm doin' here. Got a kiln over yonder and burn limestone for the lime. Use it for plasterin' and white wash."

"Maybe I can help out for awhile," replied Charles. "Seems the least I can do for your hospitality."

A few days later as Charles and Jacob were working at the kiln, Charlie called to Jacob, "You stay here. I'm goin' to Poole's blacksmith shop. Be back later this afternoon."

"Ya better be careful Charlie. You know the kind of fella's that hang around Pooles."

A couple of hours later Jacob could hear his name being called, "Jacob; Jacob, are you here?" Charles Dow was out of breath from hurrying back to their claim.

"Yeah, Charlie, I'm here. What's the matter?"

"I just spotted Coleman and Moody on my claim cutting timber."

"I suppose it's that part they claim is theirs since the new survey, huh?"

"Yeah, but it's mine. That inspection committee said it was mine and I gotta' get them off there once and for all."

"I'll go with ya Charlie, but ya better get your gun."

"No! I don't want trouble. I just want them off my land." Together they started to where Charlie had seen the men.

"Ain't no one here but me," said Moody as Branson and Dow arrived where the timber was being cut.

"I know I saw Coleman," said Charles. "He was here with you cutting my timber. You…the both of you just get off my land right now. You know they said it was mine and I want you to stay on your side of the line." Charles shook his finger in Moody's face and turned to go. "I mean it!"

Wednesday, November 21, 1855

"I'm going back to Pooles to get my parts, Jacob," said Charles. "It won't take long."

"Be careful," called Jacob. "I still think he ought to be carrying his gun with him," he muttered to himself

A short time later that day Charles Dow was headed back to his claim as he passed the home of a man named McKinney. McKinney was standing in the lane to his house talking with Frank Coleman when they noticed Charles passing by.

Coleman, who was armed, started for the road. McKinney knew right away what could happen. He had heard how Coleman and Dow had had words on several occasions and it became worse when the survey committee ruled in Dow's favor.

"Hey, Frank; wait a minute. I want to tell you something," shouted McKinney.

"Tonight," called Coleman as he continued down the lane.

"Damn Free-Stater, I'll blow every one o' ya to hell," muttered Coleman as he reached the road and raised his gun pointing at Dow's back.

The snap of the firing cap caught Dow's attention causing him to turn around. Shaking his finger at Coleman, Dow said something McKinney couldn't hear, then turned and continued down the road again.

This time there was no miss-fire. A shot rang out and Dow fell over backwards; dead. At that same time two men by the names of Buckley and Wagner were close enough down the road to see what had just happened. Later McKinney said that what ever Dow had said to Coleman must have caused Dow to be certain there would be no further trouble, "…or the durned fool wouldn't have turned his back on Coleman again."

Charles Dow's dead body lay in the dirt road until late that evening when Jacob heard about the killing and came for it. It was later said that a number of pro-slavers had passed that way during the day and had allowed the body to remain in the middle of the road.

In addition to that, when Jacob had Charlie's body back at the Branson cabin he discovered a number of bullets had been fired into the dead man during the day.

Chapter 17

Friday, November 23, 1855

Abrael had arrived at Dr. Robinson's house late in the afternoon and had been asked to spend the night. After the evening meal Abrael and Dr. Robinson were talking in the home office of the doctor.

"This murder of Dow really has me worried Abrael. I'm afraid folks aren't going to let it stop with this."

"You mean there will be more killing?" asked Abrael.

"I don't know what to think just now. After the funeral the crowd refused to break up and go home. They began to talk and behave like a violent mob." Dr. Robinson shook his head as he rose from his chair and began to move about the room.

"They wanted to burn Coleman's house and several others as well. In fact they went there, kicked in the door and got the fire started. If it hadn't been for the cool head of Sam Wood, who got some of the others to help put out the fire, the place would have been lost."

"What happened to Coleman?" asked Abrael.

"He, Buckley and several others immediately set out for Shawnee Mission so Coleman could turn himself in to Sheriff Jones and tell his side of the story first."

"I thought that Jones fella was just a post master," said Abrael with a quizzical look on his face.

"Governor Shannon appointed him Sheriff of Douglas County. That's all we need. There isn't anyone more anti Free-State than Jones. And all he needs is an excuse to start trouble for us.

"Worse yet, the next morning both Coleman's and Buckley's cabins had been burned to the ground. And I'm certain that none of our people did it. I believe that Missouri bunch did it so they could blame some of us."

Later, during the night, Abrael heard some excited voices down stairs and went to see what was happening.

"…and they tried to take him away," the nervous man was saying, "but a bunch of us blocked the road and got 'im back and then run the Sheriff off somewheres. When he left he swore that he'd be back and the town of Lawrence with all their slave lovers would be leveled." The man stopped to catch his breath and continued, "They claimed Branson was in cahoots with Dow to get Coleman and that Coleman was just acting in self defense.

"Hell Doc, Charlie didn't even have a gun on him and on top of ever' thin' he was shot in the back. Jacob tried to get him to arm himself but Charlie said it would only cause trouble."

Dr. Robinson turned to Abrael. "They tried to get Branson. They might have killed him had it not been for these folks."

The doctor turned back to the man and instructed him to gather the citizens for a meeting early the following morning.

"We got Jacob out here with us, so's he can tell his side of the story. He says he's willing to leave town if it will help settle things down."

"It's too late for that. I just wish you hadn't brought Jacob and the others to town. It's going to give Jones and Shannon the very excuse they've been looking for.

"Go on now; I've got to think!"

"I told you so, damn it; they've gone and done it and we're going to put a stop to it and anything else they think they can pull off." David Rice Atchison had brought Stringfellow and several others together and planned to raise an army that would cross the border and teach the abolitionists a lesson not soon forgotten. They would raid the arsenal at Liberty and arm themselves with rifles, ammunition and even cannons. If it was war they wanted the Missourians were ready to accommodate them.

"I've put out a call for the militia, but there is practically no response," said Governor Shannon nervously.

"They haven't had time to get really organized," replied Secretary Daniel Woodson.

"But then I contacted Fort Leavenworth and Colonel Sumner said he couldn't do anything without direct orders from the President and who knows how long that will take? And we must remember. We are only here to aid Sheriff Jones in serving his warrants. We *do not* want to be blamed for starting a war with the Free-Staters."

"Don't worry Governor; I have it taken care of. I have notified the Platte County Rifles and they will be along with D.R. and all the help we will need."

The crowd was quiet, anxious and nervous. Dr. Robinson began quietly. "We cannot afford to let the difficulties of outsiders affect our town. This is the third killing. First there was William Phillips, then Sam Collins and now Charlie Dow, besides the many who have been threatened with their lives by the Missourians. Now it has been brought to our doorstep and we are on the verge of an all out war."

"We can't let 'em run all over us," shouted James Lane. Cries of agreement went up throughout the crowd. "Lawrence must be defended or forever be ruled by the Pro-Slavery contingent from Missouri. That could lead to the Territory becoming a slave State which can not be tolerated."

Plans were set in motion to defend the town. Robinson finally agreed to become Commander in Chief if Colonel James Lane, the only one with any real military experience, would be second in command.

"We are not here to fight," reminded Robinson in a firm tone of voice. "We are here to defend our town and use every peaceable means at our disposal. If at all possible I intend to reason with Jones, the Governor and whoever else attempts to draw us into a confrontation. I intend to save Lawrence without any bloodshed what so ever if there is the slightest chance."

Lane immediately began to organize groups to set up barricades and fortify the town while Missourians crowded across the border to meet at Lecompton and also at Franklin, just below Lawrence. The more the Lawrence men became aware of the Missourians and their presence the more Lane and his aides made preparations by digging, fortifying, and drilling.

From around the Lawrence area men with military experience began to appear. It began to look more like an organized militia than a loosely formed bunch of armed people. Those not directly engaged in building the defenses were instructed to be prepared to fortify themselves in their homes and root cellars. Food and water was being stored in case the difficulty turned into a siege.

"If I don't get help soon, I'm gonna lose half my men from Missouri," complained Jones. Sheriff Jones was getting anxious. He was afraid things might cool down and he wanted his fight.

"I can't proceed without the Presidents approval," replied Governor Shannon. "How many warrants do you have to serve?"

"Around fifteen," answered Jones, "but if we wait most of the people I want will be out of the Territory!"

Sheriff Samuel Jones
Image: Kansas State Historical Society

Chapter 18

Thursday, December 6, 1855

"We're going because we are needed. Call everyone together and load into the wagon. You know what we need; we discussed it last evening." John Brown Sr. gave his orders to his son John Jr. "It is said that the Godless Missourians intend to abduct numerous citizens of Lawrence as well as destroy the printing presses and burn a number of the town's buildings. It is our job to assist in repelling this murderous horde."

There were about twenty members of the Fifth Regiment, 1st Brigade of the Kansas Volunteers commanded by Colonel George W. Smith, of which John Brown Sr. was a Captain. They would converge on Lawrence the following day.

As the Brown boys walked along next to the wagon driven by their father they formed an ominous group. The boys carried broadswords, rifles and had pistols in their belts. The top perimeter of the wagon was surrounded by knives fastened to poles held upright and reflecting the setting sun.

Upon arrival at the bridge that would carry them into Lawrence they spotted a group of what turned out to be Missourians. Abrael motioned to John Jr.

"Know them?" he asked in a whisper.

"Nope, but it doesn't matter. Father won't let them stop us if they try."

At first the Ruffians did attempt to stop the Browns, but the sight of the wagon and the many weapons leveled at them caused them to part and allow the men of the Fifth Regiment to pass, silently.

Weiner, August and Abrael had joined Brown's group as they left for Lawrence. Young Benjamin wanted to go as well but since his wife was expecting, Theodore insisted that they go stay with the Hauser's a few miles north.

Benjamin would also take two wagons filled with as many supplies as he could pack. It was a precaution and all agreed a necessary one.

Even though Dr. Robinson wanted to keep this down to just a local Lawrence affair he finally agreed it might be well to show the opposition that Lawrence would not be intimidated. The term "Wakarusa War" was being heard more and more. The people had put a name to their cause and were willing to carry out what ever effort it was going to require.

Inside the fortification at Lawrence could be seen units from all the surrounding counties and towns. In addition to the Pottawatomie Company were men from Topeka under the command of Colonel C. K. Holliday, groups from Palmyra, Ottawa Creek, Bloomington and many others.

John Brown Sr. immediately went to the Free State Hotel to coordinate with Dr. Robinson who was busy directing the Committee of Public Safety. Brown became quite upset when he was told that they were in the middle of negotiating a peaceful settlement with the opposing forces.

"I'll not believe we are willing to give in to those freedom hating barbarians from Missouri. We have God and His might on our side. We are in the right and I'll not stand by and see us kneel in such humiliation. Whether you want to call it the Wakarusa War or any other name; it is war and I have predicted it and will continue to call it war until you people are willing to admit that is exactly what it is."

Dr. Robinson tried to assure Brown that they would not be giving in to nor giving up any of their rights or freedoms.

"Nor will it be said that we committed any wrong doing. As yet we have stayed within the law as has been given to us by the Territorial Legislature and until we can change that, which we are in the process of trying to do, we will abide as best we can by those laws."

Brown stormed off with his boys determined to strike a blow of some sort to his hated enemy. "We can sneak out after dark and hit one or two of their camps," Brown confided to Owen. Word of that some how got back to Robinson who quickly ordered Brown to desist.

Abrael joined a group from Topeka that was preparing a fort-like structure of logs and dirt at the southern part of Lawrence.

"Good afternoon Judge Holliday," said Abrael as he saw C. K. Holliday approaching.

"Its Colonel now," whispered the fellow next to him.

"Oh, excuse me Colonel."

"That's fine; aren't you that friend of young Brown, Kepler is it?" asked Holliday.

"Kepper; yes Sir; I'm Abrael Kepper. We met in Topeka at the Constitutional Convention."

"That's right. Glad to have your help, Abrael."

The Colonel waved as he walked on toward some of his other workers.

"You've been to Topeka then," said the man who had spoken earlier.

"Only once," replied Abrael. "Looks like quite a place."

"Sure is; we got a saw mill, a bunch of stores and even the only ferry for miles around."

"I didn't see that," said Abrael. "That's gotta be handy."

"You bet. Two French-Canadian brothers name of Papin married two of the Kansa half-breed women so they could operate on the north side of the river. The Indians owned that land over there so that was their way around that."

Abrael laughed but agreed that it was a clever idea.

Two representatives of Dr. Robinson left late at night and arrived the next morning to have an interview with Governor Shannon. They explained that no one at Lawrence was guilty of any infraction of the Territorial laws and that they were being greatly intimidated by roving bands of Missouri bushwhackers. There had been killings, people threatened away from entering the Territory and property stolen and destroyed. They even cited the killing of Dow and explained the rescue of Jacob Branson in order to keep him from being lynched on the spot.

Governor Shannon was certain that most of the charges brought by the men from Lawrence were fabricated but finally, after much persuasion, agreed to visit Lawrence to see for himself and speak with Robinson face to face.

As the Governor's carriage approached Lawrence Shannon was shocked at the way the Missourians were behaving. They were mostly drunk, dirty and milling around exhibiting practically no discipline at all. He began to rethink his position on the matter and look more toward the peaceful people of Lawrence.

He was also ashamed to hear about the ambush and death of Thomas Barber the previous day. Barber had decided to leave Lawrence with a brother and a brother-in-law to briefly visit his wife. On the road home they were spotted by a pro-slavery patrol lead by the disreputable former Indian Agent G. W. Clarke, who gave chase ordering the men to stop. When they refused to go back with Clarke and began to ride away they were fired upon and Thomas was killed. He was the fourth recent casualty.

"I am extremely sorry *those* people have behaved in such a manner. I can assure they are not men of my choosing whatsoever. I had tried to call in the military from Fort Leavenworth as I knew they would be responsible and orderly but without the permission directly from President Pierce they could not respond," stated the Governor.

THOMAS BARBER GRAVE
LAWRENCE PIONEER CEMETERY

On through the evening it was Shannon and A. G. Boone verses Lane and Robinson hammering out an agreement with which both sides could live. Wine and other spirits dulled the hammering somewhat, at least for Shannon, to the extent that the agreement ended up a bit one sided.

The Free-Staters would abide by the laws set forth by the Territorial Legislature, which they had largely been doing all along; they would accept just judgments by the courts and would not pursue hostilities with the Missourians that had invaded their land.

The Governor, Lane and Robinson ventured under a flag of truce to the enemy headquarters where Shannon explained the gist of the treaty they were about to sign and convinced the Missourians to return home.

Back at Lawrence the finishing touches were put to the agreement. One of the "touches" late that evening was the Governor's permission for the "people" in the future to defend themselves, with weapons if necessary, against any and all armed invaders.

The Governor was called upon to re-endorse that "late touch" when he was informed that the Missourians were not ready to leave and an attack was imminent. The agreement was promptly forth coming as the Governor realized his immediate safety was at stake as well.

"Well, I guess most of the Missourians have left by now," said Abrael.

"We were fortunate to get by with no more trouble than we had," replied Dr. Robinson. "At least we had no casualties."

"I heard that the Missourians were pulling a wagon with them that had three bodies in it," said one of the by-standers.

"It was their own men and it was their own fault," said Robinson. "One of the men, I'll bet he was drunk, fell from a tree and killed himself. Another was shot by one of his own overanxious men and the third died in a fight with some of his drunken friends."

"Some friends," said Abrael.

"Anyway," said Robinson, "We are rid of them for the time being and we have a method by which we can defend our selves without breaking their law."

Soon after, when Shannon realized what he had signed, he tried to recant. He claimed he was tricked and begged to have the agreement returned. When this did not happen he immediately wrote to President Pierce trying to downplay the importance of the paper saying that it was just a temporary means for quieting an isolated incident.

In no time Sheriff Sam Jones ranted and raved about the weak, spineless Shannon who never should have settled for peace when he, Jones, had the men and weapons to wipe Lawrence from the earth. He lauded Clarke and Burns and said they should share in the honor of killing the abolitionist Barber.

And so came to an end to what later became known as the *"Wakarusa War"*; A *war* that never actually happened, although an event that was to be another solemn indication of more trouble yet to come.

COURTESY KANSAS STATE HISTORICAL SOCIETY

Chapter 19

Spring, 1856

"Boy I am glad it is finally getting to be spring. I thought winter would never end. And cold…" Abrael stood looking out at the green beginning to show in the fields and on the trees.

"We've had quite a time of it too," said August. "Just think what all has happened in the last few months.

"We adopted the Topeka Constitution and now have our own Legislature and Governor."

"I'm certainly glad Dr. Robinson was elected. I don't believe we could have done better."

"He certainly seems to know his politics and I believe he can finally get things done for the real Kansans," stated August. "The only thing that bothers me is that Pierce really has it in for Robinson and the Legislature. Remember that speech he made where he called us all traitors and said that we had committed treason? That's pretty strong talk. I'm pretty sure that if we abide by the laws and don't try to make trouble, we will be all right."

"But now we have two Governors and Legislatures. The President isn't going to allow that," replied Abrael, rather worriedly.

They busied themselves filling shelves and putting away empty boxes in the back of the store. Business was good and folks were beginning to come in from as far as twenty-five miles away.

"You read about those killings in Easton?" asked Abrael as he folded blankets to be put away in the back.

"You mean Cook?" asked August.

"Yeah; Cook got himself killed by a fella by the name of R. O. Brown. No relation to our Brown's though."

"I understand Cook was pro-slavery," offered August.

"And Brown was anti-slavery. And of course they wouldn't let it go at that so then Brown was killed by one of Cook's friends by the name of Gibson; he and some other pro-slavers."

"It's getting bad," said August, shaking his head. "There's more of that going around than we hear about too, I'll bet."

"Something's got to be done and soon," said Abrael. "John Jr. said he had written to some friends back east and told them he felt it wouldn't be long before there were a lot more killings and maybe even a war."

"Could 'a happened last year when they tried to take Lawrence," said August.

"You're right."

They each went about more chores until it was about noon. As they sat and ate their lunch Abrael leaned back in his chair and wiped his hands on his jeans.

"You've been gone August, so you probably didn't hear about the run-in Weiner had with Dutch Bill did you?"

"I heard they had words at Henry's place when they tried to get Theodore to tell them his politics," August answered.

"That's not what I'm talking about.' Abrael got a big grin on his face as he began to relate the story.

"It seems that Dutch Bill came into the store one Sunday morning when Theodore was alone. He figured he would give Weiner something to worry about.

"Well, you know Bill is about 6 foot 3 inches and around 250. That 6 foot 3 was what Bill was figuring on cause that's about 5 inches more than Weiner.

"He hadn't seen Weiner move things around like you and I have so he started in on him. First Bill made some nasty comments, and then began some shoving and finally he let loose with a punch. It never landed.

"In fact Weiner got hold of Bill and beat the tar out of him. And when he had Bill down he pulled Bill's gun from him, fired it out the door until it was empty and then threw both of them out in the dirt."

"Well I'll be jiggered," said August with a look of amazement on his face.

"Not only that," continued Abrael, "You ask Theodore about his politics now and he'll come right out and tell you that he's a Free-Stater and dares anyone to argue with him about it."

"What do you know?" smiled August. "Good for him."

"Senator Lane to Washington with Constitution".

The article in the *Kansas Freeman*, published at Topeka, by E. C. K. Garvey & Co., told of the hopes of the Kansas Legislature and the people of being finally recognized as a Free State in the Union. Not only was statehood highly desired but continuing friction between the *Bogus Legislature* and the Free-State Legislature was becoming worse.

It was rumored that warrants were being written out by the "Kansas Legislature" of 1855, naming members of the Free-State Legislature as criminals and would soon be hunted down as such.

Wednesday, April 18, 1856

" Investigative Committee Sent by Washington"

The Lawrence *Kansas Tribune* published an article stating that so much complaining had been done to the Pierce administration about the *bogus* elections that a three man committee, made up of two Republicans; John Sherman[4] and William Howard and one Democrat, Mordecai Oliver of Missouri, along with their aides were to be sent to verify the situation. In reality the Committee was already close.

"A lot of good that's going to do," said Dr. Wood. "If Pierce has anything to do with it the deck is already stacked."

"But there are two Republicans," said Abrael, who was in Lawrence to look over some cloth for Weiner's store.

"I doubt if that will count for much," said Dr. Wood, "but it is only fair to wait until we see what happens.'

About the same time more newcomers had arrived at Kansas City. *Major* Buford and his army of Georgians marched into Westport to a wild and waiting crowd lead by the all too anxious Henry Clay Pate.

H. Clay Pate was editor of the local pro-slavery *Border Star* newspaper. He had written about how the new territory was open and already being filled with settlers from all over the South. Now they would be welcoming this new group of *so-called* businessmen, tradesmen, farmers and entrepreneurs of all types.

Pate would later play a much larger part in the struggle in the Territory. In addition to constantly harassing the people of Lawrence and the surrounding area he would increase his belligerence by becoming a Missouri Militia Leader and a Deputy U. S. Marshall.

The Washington Investigating Committee watched with a puzzled eye as all of these people seemed to be rushing into the Territory and yet not taking employment or constructively adding to the development of the new promised land. Their Claims of becoming productive citizens rang hollow as their actions were being observed.

4   Brother of future General William Tecumseh Sherman

The Committee intended to make the rounds of the towns and claim owners and find out for themselves if the stories of treachery and threatened violence were a fact or just stories made up to gain leverage for their movement.

Much of the time they were closely followed by a group of "protectors", mostly from Missouri. Their presence, of course, was to clarify any questionable claims by the Free-Staters.

Back in Lawrence, Sheriff Jones made himself several arrests and then made an attempt to arrest Sam N. Wood, who had helped along with others in the rescue of Jacob Branson. When Jones approached Wood, the crowd pretended it all to be a big joke by laughing and jostling Jones and his men causing Jones to make a humiliating escape, even having his pistol stolen from him during the incident.

Jones pleaded with Governor Shannon for military support and was granted ten dragoons to assist in his hunt for the fugitives. Upon returning to Lawrence on the 23rd he found that those for whom he still had warrants had all fled. He collected those he did manage to arrest and headed back for Lecompton.

FREE STATE CONSTITUTION

TOPEKA LEGISLATURE
JANUARY 15, 1856

GOVERNOR — Charles Robinson

LIEUTENANT GOVERNOR — William Y. Roberts

SECRETARY OF STATE — Philip C. Schuyler

STATE TREASURER — John W. Wakefield

AUDITOR OF STATE — Dr. George A. Cutler

ATTORNEY GENERAL — H. Miles Moore

JUDGES OF SUPREME COURT — S. N. Latta, Morris Hunt
Martin F. Conway
REPORTER OF SUPREME COURT — E. M. Thurston

CLERK OF SUPREME COURT — Spencer H. Floyd

STATE PRINTER — John Speer

REPRESENTATIVE TO CONGRESS — Mark W. Delahay

UNITED STATES SENATORS — James Lane, A. H. Reeder

Also elected members of the State Senate and House of Representatives

Chapter 20

Monday April 21, 1856

U. S. District Judge Sterling Cato convened court at Dutch Henry's to indict several men, all free-staters, for minor infractions of the Territorial regulations. Those called to serve on the court were James and William Doyle, James Harris and Allen Wilkerson, all pro-slavery and pro-government. It was evident that the purpose of the court was to intimidate the people around Brownsville and Weinersville.

Seeing such a move coming the Browns had organized the Pottawatomie Rifles as a measure of self protection should it come to that.

"I thought this would be Mr. Brown's idea," said Abrael to Weiner as they watched John Jr. being elected Captain of the unit."

"It might have been," replied Weiner, "but the Old Man isn't about to take orders from anyone else, much less his son."

As the courtroom filled, Judge Cato could see that many of those gathered outside were members of the rifle group, but none of them were armed. The charges were read and then John Brown Jr. presented the Judge with a paper questioning the validity of the proceedings. It had been said that the Legislative Laws were not official since they were issued from Shawnee Mission and that there was a question as to whether that was the legal seat of the Legislature or not.

Disgustedly Cato read the paper, wadded it up and threw it on the floor. Shortly, Judge Cato's court was presented with another statement indicating the possible conflict that could result from the Court trying to enforce it's regulations on the people of this area.

This immediately prompted more threats of everything from

shooting, burning and general extermination of the free-staters by the Doyle's, Sherman's and others. During the next few days some of the threats were indeed carried out.

Wednesday, April 23, 1856

"I'll get 'em, by God; they wont get away from me forever." Jones had again returned to Lawrence and he was mad!

The dragoons headed by Lieutenant McIntosh were camped close to the river overlooking the town. Their presence in fact was enough to draw an occasional group of onlookers. Sheriff Jones had agreed to share a tent with the lieutenant for the night so they could get an early start the next morning.

As they were preparing for bed Jones had been outside the tent washing off when a shot rang out and Jones felt his trouser leg whip against his leg. Upon inspection Jones found a hole that had no doubt been caused by the bullet.

"That wasn't no damn stray," he cried to McIntosh. "That was meant for me."

Jones moved into his tent and stayed for several minutes before coming back out. The shot had caused the crowd to thin out some but there were still a few of the Lawrence folks brave enough to stick around to see if any real trouble would start.

Jones retired again to his tent and just before he extinguished his lantern his shadow could be seen moving around. As the result of a second shot, Jones fell to the ground next to his cot.

Soldiers, hearing the second shot rushed toward the darkness looking for the shooter and promptly stumbled over tent stakes, ropes and each other allowing the culprit to escape.

Since the Federal Investigating Committee was in Lawrence so were Dr. Stringfellow and "General" Whitfield the pro-slavery Delegate to Washington. Stringfellow was called and Jones was moved to the hotel where Stringfellow kept everyone from speaking to or seeing Jones. Later the Sheriff was moved to Lecompton, a place deemed safer and closer to Judge Lecompte and like minded people.

Whitfield raced around Lawrence proclaiming violence behind every tree and door and imploring the Investigating Committee to leave immediately, as he was about to do. He vehemently announced that it was not at all safe for them to remain in among such a vicious mob as roamed the streets of Lawrence.

"Our witnesses are afraid for their lives and will no longer appear before the men from Washington," he raved. "We must call a halt to this meeting at once. No doubt the Committee has seen enough to know the deplorable conditions we are forced to be exposed to."

Whitfield left town; the Committee stayed.

The morning after Jones was shot the Lawrence citizens met to voice their disapproval of the shooting and offered any assistance that would be beneficial.

Charles Robinson wrote a letter to be delivered to Colonel E. V. Sumner expressing his regret that such a cowardly attack had taken place. He assured the Colonel that Lawrence would do all in its power to assist in apprehending the shooter. He even advised that the Lawrence Committee of Safety had offered a reward for the capture of Jones' assailant.

General Whitfield returned to Lawrence just in time to assure the Investigating Committee he had been called away concerning another disturbance and he had not been scared away from town. The Committee paid little mind.

Judge S. D. Lecompte had indeed issued warrants for Robinson, Lane, Reeder and a number of others connected with and elected to the Free-State Legislature.

U. S. Deputy Marshall Fain tried unsuccessfully to arrest the former governor and now *Senator* Reeder, as Reeder was testifying before the Committee.

"I'm not required to honor your warrant," he replied. "I have special immunity due to my position as a Senator." Looking to the Committee members for assistance, for the moment Reeder received none.

Fain continued his search for Lane and Robinson and on the following day returned to Reeder with a contempt order which Reeder also declined to accept.

Upon fearing his imminent arrest and at the suggestion of his friend John Sherman, Governor Robinson and his wife boarded a steamboat for as far to the east as they could manage and remain undetected. They made it as far as Lexington, Missouri where the Governor was arrested, taken off the boat and later ended up in the prison at Camp Sackett close to Lecompton; a place that would soon hold John Brown Jr., Representative Henry H. Williams and many others.

Reeder, also concerned that his luck would not hold, convinced the Committee to allow him to leave for Washington under the pretext of delivering some of the Committee's reports. That left Lane along with other members of the Free-State Legislature.

Lane had managed to leave Lawrence and was touring back East enlisting sympathy and gathering potential Free-State settlers.

The Investigating Committee finally headed back to Weston, then to Washington to make their reports which would be pro and con for both sides of the Territorial question.

It was noted that included among the writs were warrants also for the two Lawrence newspapers and the Free-State Hotel. The newspapers were charged with publishing pro-abolitionists articles which was strictly against the Territorial laws. In fact it was against the law to even openly speak against the Pro-Slavery Government or its purposes.

The hotel, constructed by the Immigrant Aid Society, was considered by the Legislature a fortress rather than just a hotel. It was claimed that it was built to withstand an invasion, which suggested there might be one, which implied Lawrence expected trouble. And since the Territorial Government planned no aggressive action it followed that the aggression must be planned by those in Lawrence. Hence their aggressive fortress must come down.

And apparently the plan was in the works.

THE "MUSTANG" TEAM

Brother Jonathan at Union Toll Gate: "No Sir-ee! you can't come any such load over us."

Horace Greeley, *New York Tribune*: "Come my good People open the Gate its all right! We are the true Union Party because we ride on the wooly horse (abolitionism)."

James G. Bennett, *"Herald"*; "Ever since I mounted behind the old white Coated Philosopher (Greeley) I find that everything he says can be re-lied on."

Henry J. Raymond *"New York Times"*; "Except when he calls me "little Villain" and then he can't be re-lied on."

John C. Freemont (Republican Presidential Candidate); "There seems to be something in the road, but those fellows on the Horse, will swear me through anything; so I'll keep mum." (Mrs. Freemont rides in the back of the wagon.)

James W. Webb *"Courier & Enquirer"*; "Hurry up there Horace! or [Southern Democrat Preston S.?] Brooks will be running his
Express Train into us; I've had one ride on his Cowcatcher lately, and I don't want another"
A ragged boy shouts to the driver, "Cut behind."

Chapter 21

Tuesday May 20, 1856

"You say he's all right Dr. Wood?" asked Abrael.

"Yes, Son, I doubt it was near as serious as they let on. Jones is strutting around just like his old self."

"Has anyone heard anything from the committee yet?"

"No and I doubt that it will make much difference when we do." Dr. Wood paused to look around as he and Abrael walked down Massachusetts Street in the center of Lawrence. The tall brick Free State Hotel stood on the corner casting its shadow toward the eastern side of the street.

"Ever looked inside there Abrael?" asked Dr. Wood motioning toward the hotel.

"No Sir," replied Abrael, "but I will some day just out of curiosity."

"Nice place; big too. And you can see a long way from the top floor. Even farther from the roof, so I'm told by the workmen. The place is due to open tomorrow. Supposed to be a big ceremony I hear."

They walked past the newspaper and across to the druggist. Dr. Wood bought some laudanum and a roll of wide white bandages.

"Glad you came to town, Abrael. I missed you last time you were here. And you must promise to stay at our house tonight so you can tell me all about your store and how things are going down your way."

"It is nice of you to ask, Doctor, but I will have to leave by noon tomorrow, if I'm going to get back by dark."

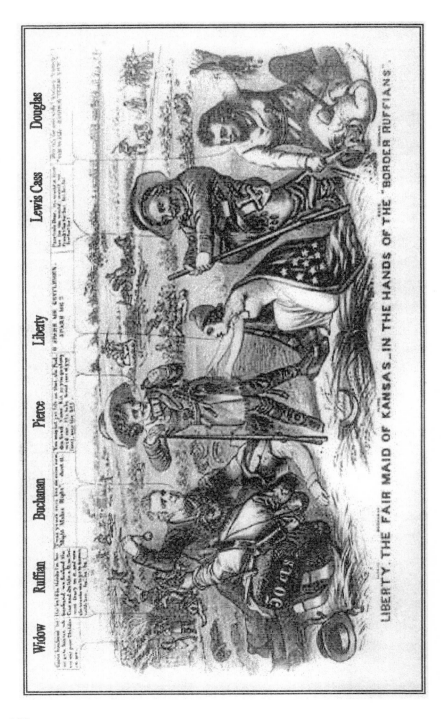

LIBERTY, THE FAIR MAID OF KANSAS IN THE HANDS OF THE "BORDER RUFFIANS"

Widow: "Come Husband, let us go to heaven, where our poor Children are."

Ruffian: "Ho! ho! She thinks I'm her husband, we Scalped the Cus and she like a D——m fool went Crazy on it, and now she wants me to go to heaven with her..."

Buchanan: "T'was once yours but its mine now, "Might makes right," don't it."

Pierce: "You may bet your life on that, ole Puddinhead," "Come Sis—sy, you go along wid me, I'le take Good care of "you" (hic) over the left."

Liberty: "O spare me gentlemen, spare me!!"

Lewis Cass; "Poor little Dear. We wouldn't hurt her for the world, would we Frank? ha! ha! ha!..."

Douglas; "Hurrah for our side! Victory! Victory! We will subdue them yet."

1856 Cartoon: A bitter indictment of the Democratic administration's responsibility for violence and bloodshed in Kansas in the wake of the Kansas-Nebraska Act.

As Abrael entered the Wood's living room the following morning he saw all the family at the window looking off toward the southwest.

"What is it?" inquired Abrael.

"Trouble I'll bet." Dr. Wood pointed to the top of Mount Oread. There were hundreds of men assembled and the morning sun reflected off the barrels of several cannon; all pointed toward the town.

"I knew it. We spoke of it at the meeting two days ago. The Missourians have been congregating all around the area for several days. Just a couple of weeks ago Fain came to town again looking for more of our people."

"What did you do about it?" asked Abrael.

"Just what we agreed we'd do. Nothing! We said we would cooperate with the authorities unless we were attacked or threatened and so far it hasn't come to that."

"Oh no?" said Mrs. Wood. "With all those hoodlums wandering around carrying guns and shoving decent folks off the sidewalks, what do you call it?"

"We sent a letter to the Governor asking for some military protection, Abrael, but all we got was a letter from Marshall Donaldson saying that most of the unrest was coming from the citizens of Lawrence. He claimed Jones told him we wouldn't allow him to serve his warrants. And here we even offered to help when we could."

Dr. Wood moved away from the window. "We have bent over backwards to avoid even any appearance of improper behavior. We told them the border ruffians were forming and starting to patrol the roads into Lawrence."

"Tell him about the Jones boy," said Mrs. Wood as she removed her apron.

"The lad was on his way to his mother's place when he was stopped and then shot for some unknown reason."

"And then," broke in Mrs. Wood, "when two men went to get the boy's body one of them was shot and killed. You know what Jones did? Nothing! Not a thing; said he had no witnesses or details so his hands were tied."

"There have been more killings than most people know about," said Dr. Wood in a subdued voice.

"I can't believe such a thing," said Abrael, then paused and continued, "I guess I can, really. We have been given warnings down at Weinersville too. Buford's men have been making all sorts of threats and the Doyle's have been going around telling people they have a week to leave or else. They tell everyone that their property and maybe even their lives are at risk. Most of our people don't scare easily but any more we have to move around in groups and we don't dare leave our stock unattended."

"I had no idea, Son. It's that bad there too, eh?"

"Last evening Fain was here again and got two more of our men. We agreed at the town meeting we wouldn't object as long as no one was harmed, but now I want you," Dr. Wood nodded at his wife, "to go next door and get Mrs. Evans and her children and go to the church basement like we talked about." Again he looked to the top of Oread. "I'll come get you when I think it is safe."

"Come on Abrael. As long as you're here you might as well join with us. Perhaps your cool head may come in handy."

Together they walked the few blocks to the center of town where the Committee of Safety generally met.

Around noon Marshall Fain and about a dozen men rode into town. They gathered another dozen or so citizens and informed them that they were now part of his posse and they were going to arrest a few more "of yer fine city fathers."

Fain, with his rough talk and manner was hoping to get the people riled up so he could use it as an excuse to attack the town as they had planned. Instead the people went along as directed and located three on Fain's list.

The prisoners were put under guard while Fain and the rest of his original group "opened" the dining room of the Free State Hotel and had a free lunch. When they finished they walked out, got in their wagons and buggies and left, headed for Oread.

In an hour or so a large contingent of men and several cannon could be seen slowly descending Mount Oread. Riding out ahead of them, still a little wobbly on his horse, came Sheriff Jones with about two dozen men.

"Pomeroy at the hotel?" yelled Jones as he road up Massachusetts Street. When he reached the front of the building the door opened and Samuel Pomeroy stepped into the street.

"What do you want Jones?"

"That's Sheriff Jones, "General"," said Jones with a chuckle in his voice.

"Of course, Sheriff, how is your back?"

"Never mind the soft soap; now I'm gonna tell ya just what I want and you've got about ten minutes to see we get it or else the whole town goes up."

"Yes Sheriff; just tell me what you want."

"I want every weapon ya got and I want 'em piled right here in the middle of the street."

"Sir, I will give you what little we have; …that is what the Committee has. We have one small cannon that we keep at the store over there and a hand full of small arms and ammunition. That is all."

"What about all the rifles and such I been hearin' about?"

"Sheriff what you have heard I'm certain has been exaggerated and what few there are, are privately owned and I have no authority to force the citizens to give them up unless they are breaking the law."

"Look behind you Abrael," said Dr. Wood, pulling at Abrael's arm.

Just then the street was filled with men on horseback, waving rifles and pistols. It was easy to tell they had been drinking. The yelling and firing in the air began as the townsmen drew back into doorways and around corners. Several of the cannon were maneuvered into various positions and in the center of the Missourians rode David Rice Atchison, Stringfellow and Buford. Atchison could hardly seat his horse.

"Not one damn abolitionist has dared to raise even a pop gun. By God, 'Southern Rights' has won the damn day and we didn't have to fire a shot," yelled Atchison.

"But we're about to," replied Buford with big grin on his face.

Abrael stood almost at a loss for words. Finally he turned to Dr. Wood. "Aren't the people going to do something? Are we just going to stand here…why aren't we…?"

"Hush," said Dr. Wood in a low tone. "We promised we wouldn't do anything to give them a reason to claim we defied the law. They will say that this isn't an attack on the city because they have warrants."

"But we can't just let them…" At that Abrael pushed his way through the crown toward one of the men pushing at the cannon. "You can't just blow up our hotel. Who do you think…?"

At that point the man turned and struck Abrael on the side of his head with the back of his hand. Abrael went down to one knee. With a solid blow to the Missourian's stomach Abrael regained his feet. Just then Dr. Wood and two other men grabbed Abrael and dragged him toward the sidewalk.

"I'll get you, you little Jew bastard," cried the man at the cannon. At that point one of the other Missourians yelled, "C'mon Ezra grab hold here."

The first cannon was aimed at the *Free State* newspaper building and fired point blank without a word of warning. Luckily no one inside was injured. The border ruffians smashed through the windows and front door and began to spill type on the floor and pull down the shelves. The press was roped and dragged out into the street and down toward the river.

The printing paper had been set ablaze and smoke spewed out of the windows, door and hole the cannon had produced. Ink was poured all over the front of the building and was causing footprints to appear along the street.

Next was the *Herald of Freedom* paper. It suffered the same treatment. Everything was ruined in minutes and the building was disappearing in smoke and falling debris.

"Stand back," bellowed Atchison as he staggered toward one of the cannon. "I'm gonna test the strength of that there fortress. We'll see if they build 'em like we do in Missouri."

He pulled the cannon barrel toward the hotel as best he could and held his cigar to the touch hole.

The cannon exploded, rolling back about a foot, nearly taking Atchison with it. The cannon ball missed the entire building completely.

"What kind o' damn equipment ya got here? What's wrong......" Then Atchison began to laugh. He stood with one hand on the cannon barrel and looked around at his men as they all began to laugh. "Okay, you bunch of Kickapoo Rangers, let's get that damn thing down."

At that the cannons were loaded, aimed and fired. It was a little disappointing that the damage was considerable less than expected. Still the firing continued. Bricks were dislodged and glass broken. Doors were blown off their hinges and finally when the cannons were abandoned, men were sent streaming inside and up the stairs to pitch furniture through the windows and down the stairways.

It wasn't long before it was found out that the basement was what needed to be cleared out first. Wine and whiskey bottles and even cases were dragged into the street and passed around. Tar was poured into the rooms and hallways to help the fire when it got a good start. Gun powder that had been brought for the cannons was placed inside the building but did little more than break more windows.

With the building finally in flames in places a voice was heard, "Looks like we got our job done, boys. Your work is finished."

It was more like, "this part is finished; now do what ever else you want to", and the looting and destruction took on new meaning. Anything the Missourians took a fancy to was taken while the townspeople stood and watched. Men gritted their teeth as they saw their town being ransacked. Still they remained true to their word and as they had pledged, refrained from resisting. They just stood there watching the hotel walls began to crumble.

One unlucky border ruffian just happened to be standing too close. A brick from the upper section of the hotel fell, hit him on the head and killed him.

"Dr. don't you call this being attacked?" begged Abrael. "Why don't they fight back now?"

The doctor just shook his head and pulled Abrael further back from the crowd.

The finishing touch was the firing and destruction of the house on the hill. Governor Robinson's home was reduced to ashes. It was finished. Women and children came up from the basements and ravine just west of town.

At least there were no Lawrence citizens hurt except for broken hearts. Yet they were not beaten. They had not yielded and had not been caused to raise their fist or break their word. No Territorial Law had been broken by one Lawrence Free-Stater. But that would soon change.

In the ensuing months, Free-State bands of raiders robbed and pillaged the Pro-Slavery settlers without mercy. No one, regardless of their politics was safe now. And it was only going to get worse. Burnings and killings increased up and down the Kansas-Missouri border. Soon the land along both sides of the state line was practically desolate. Both Kansas and Missouri was bleeding badly.

The Sacking of Lawrence May 21, 1856

Courtsey Kansas Historical Society

Chapter 22

Monday, May 21, 1856

"We got word late last night. They're about to really do it this time," Brown Jr. was told. "The Border Ruffians are massing outside Lawrence a thousand strong, with rifles and cannons. It looks like they mean business and will not be stopped."

"We must go," declared John Brown Jr. "It is time for the Pottawatomie Rifles to defend its land." John Jr., a member of the Topeka Legislature, had been elected Captain of the unit and called together as many of the men as he could on such short notice.

Theodore Weiner, also a member, retrieved his rifle, small hunting knife and as much ammunition as he could carry in his pockets. He also had a small bag of lead he placed in the back of the wagon they were taking.

They moved out around four o'clock in the afternoon, marching for about two miles, and then resting until nearly dark. They finished their march under a last quarter moon reaching a point on Ottawa Creek just south of Ottawa Jones' cabin.

The following day around noon the Brown party received the report on Lawrence.

"I'm afraid we've got some bad news." Abrael and a messenger heading south delivered the word that Lawrence was a lost cause.

"Just what do you mean?" asked John Brown Sr.

"Yesterday about a thousand Missourians and their Kansas friends blew up and burned the Free State Hotel. There is nothing left but a bunch of ashes and one brick wall."

"Also," said Abrael, "both newspapers were destroyed. The presses are in the river, the paper burned and the type and other equipment badly damaged or gone altogether."

"And just who…?"

"It was all of them; Atchison, Buford, Jones and I don't know who all else," replied Abrael.

"How many were killed?" asked John Sr. "What about the women and children?"

Abrael looked at the other messenger and then back to Brown. "No one was killed... that is except one of Buford's men had a brick fall on his head and kill him. That was it."

"But how can that be? I don't understand!" growled Brown.

"The people didn't fight back," said Abrael quietly.

"You mean they just stood there and took it? They didn't lift a finger to stop these...these..."

"No Sir," said Abrael. "They had pledged themselves not to break any of the Territorial Laws by fighting or going against the judge's ruling."

"What ruling do you mean?" asked John Jr, stepping forward.

"Judge Lecompte issued warrants for not only some of the people, and you are one of the wanted, but they also had warrants allowing them to destroy the newspapers because they write...wrote, articles condoning anti-slavery."

"But the hotel...?"

"They said it was a fortress intended for the use in war. And since they claim that the only troublemakers are the Free-Staters, it was condemned as well."

"I've never heard of such a thing."

"And the people just stood there and took this humiliation? Nothing but a bunch of cowards!" stuttered Brown Sr. between clenched teeth. "Cowards!"

"Well, what do we do now?" asked Weiner.

"I say we keep going," said John Jr. "We may still be needed. It's hard to tell what those Missourians will do now. They just might decide to continue on to Topeka or even head this way."

"I'm going back with you!" stated Abrael. His disappointment had returned to anger.

Having been joined by more volunteers they proceeded on to about four or five miles south of Palmyra where they spent the night.

Around noon of the following day, the 23rd, Brown Sr. told the men he had received word that there was trouble back at Pottawatomie and that they needed to turn back. At this point the group broke up and most headed home.

The senior Brown, H. H. Williams, now in charge of the Pottawatomie Rifles, Weiner and Brown Jr. stood off by themselves talking. Williams, who was the most familiar with the surrounding territory was seen to hand Brown Sr. a paper with what looked like a list of names written on it.

"Townsley," called Brown Sr. "come here."

After a few words Townsley was heard to say, "....but I don't think I want to. You know they threatened to kill us all..."

Brown raised his voice to him and gave him to understand that he had no choice. "Something must be done!"

Brown needed Townsley's wagon so Townsley was forced to accompany Brown and the others back toward the Pottawatomie; but apparently on a different mission.

"What's going on Theodore?" asked Abrael.

"Never mind; you head back home and look after things until I get there."

"But why can't..."

"Hier raus, schnell!"

What's...?"

"*I said* never mind!" Weiner shook Abrael by the shoulders. "Just do as I say. I'll explain when I get home! That is, whatever home we have left."

Chapter 23

Sunday, May 25, 1856

Late Sunday morning Abrael finally found Weiner behind the barn wiping down his pony.

"Where've you been Theodore? I've been looking for you all morning."

"I've been around," stated Weiner in a quiet voice.

"There was a man here earlier; came ridding in like the devil was after him. He said there had been a mass killing on the Pottawatomie. He said five men had been killed; three of them the Doyles." Abrael paused. "They're blaming the Browns."

Abrael looked at Theodore. Then he reached out and touched Theodore's shirt. "What's that?" Abrael rubbed the dark stain on Theodore's sleeve.

"Come on, I'll tell you. You're gonna hear pretty soon any way and you need to hear the real story."[5]

"There were eight of us all together," began Weiner. "There was Capt. Brown, Salmon, Frederick, Owen, Watson and Oliver and then Henry (Thompson) and me.

"After I sent you home Friday, we went south, camped, and then late Saturday night we headed for the Doyle's place. We stopped at someone's cabin on the way but we didn't know whose it was for sure and there was no one home anyway.

---

5   The following account is based on the <u>sworn testimony</u> of James Townsley given to Judge James Hanway later during an official investigation and upon sworn statements by John Brown Jr, Mrs. Doyle and Mrs. Wilkinson.

"I was on my pony while all the rest were in Townsley's wagon. There was only a little bit of moon and it was hard to see where we were going.

"Captain Brown said we should make as little noise as possible. He also said that while he knew how we felt about killing we were required to go after our deadly enemies. And because of the killings, threats of more killings and beatings that had taken place against our people we had to 'strike terror into the hearts of the pro-slavery party' or we could all perish."

Weiner stopped, took a long breath, and slowly and quietly continued.

"We finally got to the Doyle's cabin. Frederick, Townsley and I waited with the wagon. I think Brown was afraid Townsley would run if he got the chance. The rest went to the cabin and knocked on the door.

"About this time one of Doyle's big dogs came at us out of the dark; scared hell out of me. Fred took a swipe at him with his broad sword and Townsley got 'im with his saber. That was the end of him.

"Then Frederick and Townsley were sent on to Dutch Henry's to make sure they were going to be there cause Brown had them in mind as well. Then we were all supposed to meet up at Harris' place, which we did.

"Brown pounded on Doyle's door. When Doyle answered from inside one of the Browns asked where Wilkinson lived. Doyle said he would tell them and opened the door. Brown and a couple of the boys went inside and Brown told Doyle that he represented the army and that he was to come with him. I guess Brown was figuring that since he was the head of part of the militia that qualified him as representing the army.

"Anyway Mrs. Doyle really started in on her husband telling him that she had said that his carryin' on with Buford, Cato and that bunch was going to get him in trouble and now here it was. She was really mad. Doyle told her to shut up but that didn't stop her.

"Then she began to beg for the Browns not to take young John Doyle because he was only seventeen and didn't do anything.

"At first the Doyle's weren't going to come out so someone, I think it was Thompson, began to make it look like we were going to burn down the cabin. That seemed to convinced Doyle so he and his two oldest sons, the ones that were going around with him making threats and nailing up eviction signs, that was William and Drury Doyle, they came out and they all went off toward the creek.

"Salmon said they tried to make short work of it. But we heard a couple of screams when they were hit with the swords. I guess one of the Doyle boys tried to get away and they had to run him down. They were all done in by the boys and their broad swords. That's what they said when they came back.[6]

"From there we headed to Wilkinson's place. We knocked on the door and asked the directions to Dutch Henry's. At first he said he would tell us from inside and refused to come out. Then Brown asked him if he wasn't a pro-slaver and of course since he was a member of the legislature he had to say that he was. We forced our way in and found Mrs. Wilkinson sick in bed with the measles.

"Wilkinson said he couldn't leave her and said he would not run if they'd let him get help for her. I guess he promised he would still be there the next morning but they didn't trust him so Thompson and I took him out away from the house quite a ways and used the broad swords on him too." Weiner didn't look up when he told that part to Abrael in a rather lowered voice.

---

6   Mrs. Doyle claimed her husband was shot in the head. Later several persons said that Doyle did have a bullet hole in the back of his head. John Brown Jr. denied the fact since he stated that it would have been for no purpose since Doyle was already dead and his father wanted no gunfire to call attention to what they were doing.

"Well, any way, we all met up again on the way to Harris' place. It was just up from Dutch Henry's. When we got there we hammered on the door and forced our way inside.

"We found Mr. and Mrs. Harris there with three others; one of them was Dutch Bill! The others were John Wightman and Jerome Glanville.

"Captain Brown goes in wanting to know just who all these people were and who was pro-slavery and who was free-state. Mr. and Mrs. Harris were in bed and there was such a commotion it was hard to tell what was happening.

"When the men were gathered together Brown says he represents the northern army and was here to take charge and it would do no good to resist.

"The first one that was taken out to be questioned was someone that even Harris didn't know. Actually his name was Glanville. He was just visiting and staying overnight. He had bought a cow from Dutch Henry, who knows whose cow it might have been," said Weiner with a chuckle. It seemed he was trying to lighten the telling just a bit.

"Well he didn't know anything about any raids and so we figured he couldn't have been in on any of the trouble and sent him back into the house.

"The next fella was Harris himself. It turned out he didn't know anything either. He said he had just come to this part of the country because he could make a better living here than anywhere he tried. He told us where we could get some saddles and bridles along with some of Dutch Henry's horses and we sent him back in the house too.

"We asked about old Dutch Henry but they said he was somewhere out on the prairie rounding up some stock. Captain Brown was really put out about that. He wanted Henry and Judge George Wilson really bad but it just didn't work out, lucky for them

"Next it was Dutch Bills' turn. He wasn't so lucky.

Every one, including me, knew where he stood and all the threats he had made. He had scared hell out of all the free-state settlers around here but me. He had it coming and he got it!"

"Golly, Theodore," said Abrael. "I had no idea it was going to be like that."

Theodore leaned forward, placed his hand on Abrael's knee. "You haven't heard the best part!"

"When folks hear this, it will make them look at this all together differently.

"At the Harris place, when we got inside and before Mrs. Harris knew what was really happening, she went into the kitchen and began to get the stove ready to start cooking. She was so busy she wasn't paying much attention to anything else going on.

"Then her husband went over to her and asked her just what the hell she was doing?"

"You told me just yesterday," she says to him, "that just as soon as these men showed up I was to fix them breakfast cause they were going to be hungry and had a big job to do."

"Woman, just who do you think these men are?'

"You said Buford's men were coming and I...'[7]

"These are John Brown and his men! They are probably going to kill us all. These are the people the Henry's have been going on about. They are all Free-Staters!"

"You see Abrael; we just beat them to it! Buford and his men are ready with a long list of people they are going to kill and run out of the country. They've been planning this for weeks. It isn't just a spur of the moment thing like we did. They have been gathering their

[7]   From a letter from Hon. James Hanway to James Redpath of the *New York Tribune*, March 12, 1860.

forces, and supplies and choosing names for their list; it's a plan of attack just like in a real war.

"Remember how Wilkinson, just three or four days ago was going around saying that in a few days some of the free state men would either be dead or run out of the country?

"Come to find out, according to what we learned from this, we were just a day or two ahead of them and they weren't ready to stop at five or six or even ten. I'll bet that you and me, the Browns and everyone around here are on their list; and may still be. All we can hope for is that what we did will make them think twice and let them know we aren't going to be running scared. We have proved that!"

Weiner paused, leaned back and looked at Abrael. "Well, there it is. Now you see why I didn't want you there? I have no idea what will happen to all of us now, but maybe, just maybe those ruffians and claim jumpers will think twice before they cause any more trouble.

"I tell you Abrael; the people around here won't stand for any more threats and they won't run any more. It's time for us to do something to let them know we mean business. I think most everyone is with us and know that if we stand together we will win." [8]

---

8   See Page 173 for "Comments made later concerning the Pottawamie Massacre".

Chapter 24

Monday, May 26, 1856

Brown and his men had decided to go to Jason Brown's claim on Brown's Branch. Brown strode ponderously alone around the timber contemplating what his next move might be.

In the morning of May 22nd, the day before the Pottawatomie incident, Senator Charles Sumner of Massachusetts had been badly beaten on the floor of the U. S. Senate for his bitter speech, *"The Crime against Kansas"*. It is not known for certain if Brown was able to get the news of the attack this soon however he was acquainted with Sumner and had spoken to him on at least one occasion and greatly admired his work.

"John Jr. swears there's gonna be a regular war," stated Abrael. "He even referred to a *civil war* in one of his letters to his father some time ago. Do you really think that could happen? I mean, a whole country go to war over slavery? After all it's been going on for years now."

"Abrael, you know as much about the fight for personal freedom as anyone. We Jews have been at it for centuries and frankly I can't see any way around it here either... sooner or later," said Weiner.

'We've all hadda' do some fightin' for our homes one way or another," said Jacob Cantrell, as they sat watching Old Brown. "I was told them Missourians would have me dead if it took twenty years," Jacob went on.

"What on earth for?" asked Abrael. "I knew you were from Missouri but I didn't know you left because someone was after you."

"I didn't," replied Jacob. "We left last year because we wanted a new start and didn't wanna be caught up with them pro-slavers." Cantrell pulled one leg under the other as he sat on the grass and played with a dandelion. "In fact we built the first cabin in Palmyra. We had to live in the wagon until I got a roof on it and even then we didn't have no floor or even a door.

"We had bugs, snakes and rats. Would you believe the wolves would wander in at night and sniff around? Our daughter Mary Jane was scarred t'death after dark."

"So, why were the folks in Missouri mad at you?" asked Abrael.

"Well, after we were here for a spell I went back to where I used to live to get some tools and other b'longings. I knew I probably shouldn't have but I figured I'd show 'em and I painted "Kansas Free State" on the side of the wagon canvas.

Abrael looked over at Townsley and then back to Jacob.

"I said it was probably a dumb thing t' do but anyway as we were leaving to come back a bunch of guys rushed out and grabbed the team and held them while another took a big ol' butcherin' knife and ripped the canvass all t' pieces." Jacob squirmed around a little, "like t' scarred m'wife and daughter out a' their minds. They said they get me if'n it took twenty years.

"And they've been true t' their word. My wife has seen several of 'em around town a number of times and I even had to hide in the woods a couple of days once."

"I had no idea you were having that kind of trouble Jacob. You know that if you ever......."

"Yeah, I know Abrael, and I appreciate it but we've all had some bad times and that's why if'n there's a fight I intend to be right in the middle of it!"

The morning of the 28th brought even more staggering news. This was literally the match to the fuse.

Ben Cochrane, one of Brown's Pottawatomie Rifles rode into camp and stopped directly in front of Brown Sr.

"What kind of trouble is it?" asked Brown as he recognized the look on Ben's face.

"It's gone; that is most everything is." He paused for a breath as he dropped the reigns and pulled off his hat. "They came in a bunch and they first burned Bondi's cabin and then went after Weiner's store. They took most of the goods they could carry and drove off the live stock."

"But I thought Captain Cook's Dragoons were there on guard," said Brown raising his voice.

"They was there but all they did was watch. Cook said he couldn't do nuthin' lest he had orders. The onlyst thing he did was make 'em leave the prisoners they tried to take."

"Was it Buford and his bunch?" asked Old Brown.

"Bet it was," said one of the younger Browns. "Remember when we went right into their camp pretending to be surveyors and got them to tell us all about what they were gonna do and who all they were gonna run off and kill?"

"Yeah and remember how they almost beat poor Mr. Manace to death just for readin' a paper they said was for abolition; then made 'im leave his place, too!"

"No," said Ben. "It wasn't Buford; it was that other fella name o' Cook, with his men from Bates County over in Missouri. They was lots of 'em, all over ever' where.

"Oh yeah; they got old Mr. Morris too fer supplyin' you folks with lead fer yer bullets."

"Wilkinson said they were going to get everyone of us in the area sooner or later," said August as he stood with tears of rage running down his dark face.

"The Doyles' said the same thing," agreed Theodore Weiner. "They came around threatening all of us if we didn't leave and they put up that warning on my store. They threatened old man Morse, that fella that had the store over by Dutch Henrys; told him to leave in five days or him and his family would be dead. They claimed to have warrants from Judge Cato and said to git out or else." Weiner sighed and shrugged his shoulders.

"But, at least we managed to save some of our things," Weiner said as he looked down at his worn hands. "The couple of wagons we filled with supplies and sent with Benjamin are left anyway. I had a feeling this would happen someday."

Brown stood quietly, then turned without another word and walked toward the trees. All the rest remained silent as well. There was nothing to say. At least the women folk had been sent to safety before the men had left.

"But that ain't all," continued Ben. "Jones's got a warrant out for John Jr., Jason and several others. Claims they was the ones what did the killin' on the Pottawatomie. If'n they catch 'em they'll hang 'em sure as hell."

A local farmer by the name of A. O. Carpenter had entered the camp and asked for Old Brown. As they talked Carpenter told him that it was rumored that there were Missourians out looking for Brown and his men.

"We've already heard about some of them," replied Brown.

"They say that these here fella's are somewhere near Black Jack, close to Captain's Creek. I know the area and I can show ya."

Brown said something to Weiner then headed to where his sons were gathered watching their father.

Weiner motioned to Abrael. "Come on. We're going huntin'."

Brown and his four sons, along with Thompson, Weiner, Kepper, Bondi and Townsley agreed to follow Carpenter. "It had come to this, finally," Brown thought to himself. "It is out of my hands now. This is the work of Providence. I must be certain in my mind that we are on God's side."

As the men readied themselves for sleep, Abrael saw one of the younger men reading a letter. The paper was worn and seemed to have had plenty of use.

The young man looked up and noticed Abrael watching him.

"From my girl up in Leavenworth," he said with a slight grin. "Haven't been able to get up there to see her for quite a spell."

"Gee, that's too bad," replied Abrael.

"Well, maybe soon if things quiet down I can make it. Her father doesn't cotton to anti-slavery folks and I can't seem to get it in my head that ownin' another person and makin' 'em do my work is right."

Abrael nodded as the young man went back to re-reading his letter for the twentieth time.

Abrael had no one to write to except the men back at the store in Leavenworth and that just didn't seem to be the same. For the first time in a long time he felt a slight twinge of loneliness. He occasionally missed having a family but he had been so busy trying to find his niche in life that a family…a girl…hadn't seemed very important. Now he had a place a little more settled, at Weiner's, and the possibility of becoming a teacher.

Suddenly it came to him. He didn't have a place any more. He still had the land, probably, but the cabin and all his possessions were destroyed. Just like his ancestors, he was homeless and alone again.

But he wouldn't be beaten! He had started without much before and he could again. Only this time he would put up a fight for it. He would not be denied. He would have a home, a family and he would teach; somehow, someway!

They camped the next morning near a spring on Ottawa Creek not far from Prairie City. It was here that James Redpath actually stumbled upon Brown's camp and joined the party. Redpath was a newspaper man from back East that had taken upon himself the task of representing the Free-Staters of the Kansas Territory.

Redpath had been spotted as an intelligent and very capable reporter by Horace Greeley, editor of the New York "Tribune", and was hired to report on the slavery situation in the South. Greeley had also hired a reporter by the name of W. A. Phillips that found his way to Kansas but his whereabouts at the time were unknown.[9]

In 1856, Redpath came to Kansas to cover what he felt was the violent and potentially explosive political situation. Finding Brown was a streak of extremely good fortune.

Captain Shore, of the Prairie City Rifles, having been told of the men's whereabouts arrived at Brown's camp early the following Saturday with some additional information about the Missourians.

"I figured I'd find somebody here," said Shore. "There have been horses and personal goods stolen from the folks near Willow Springs. They want to know what's gonna be done about it!" Shore paused and looked around. "If you're gonna handle it I can tell ya that the men you're looking for are camped at Black Jack Springs a few miles east of Palmyra."

"How many of your men can we count on?" asked Brown.

"Well, ya see, my fellers aren't that wild about goin' off and leavin' their places unguarded," said Shore with an almost whinny tone in his voice.

"But you are willing for me to risk my men," stormed Brown as he turned and walked toward the woods.

Shore stood for a moment and then left but surprisingly returned later that afternoon with a few provisions. He had discussed the raid on the Missourians with his men and some of them reluctantly, out of shame no doubt, agreed to join with Brown's group.

A discussion followed ending in a plan for Brown and his men to meet up with Shore and his people the next morning, June 1st, at Prairie City.

"Looks like we may be in for some action, you suppose?" asked Abrael.

---

9   W. A. Phillips would go on to help found the city of Salina, Kansas.

"Yeah, and I'm not so certain it's such a good idea," replied Townsley.

He had acted nervously ever since Brown had approached him about searching out the Missourians. Abrael wondered about Townsley's dedication to their task at hand. Everyone else had been ready to do what ever it was going to take to make the Missourians stay on their side of the border. Kansans had their hands full deciding what their future would be without outside interference.

Being Sunday morning the local citizens had gathered at Prairie City which consisted of very little with the main structure in town being a log cabin about twenty by twenty. They were to meet with an itinerate preacher for services and then discuss the threats that had been made against them by the Missourians. The cabin was packed with worshipers. The womenfolk filled the small structure while the men, well armed due to the prevailing circumstances, crowded around the door outside. As the men strained to hear the preacher, they suddenly heard and saw three riders approaching.

As the riders came abreast of the cabin something caused one of the horses to stumble and throw his rider to the hard packed dusty road. As his two companions stop to help, several of the men from the church ran to the fallen stranger and demanded to know who he and the other two men were.

After menacing looks and loud demands the men admitted to being members of H. Clay Pate's Missouri Militia. Prior to this Pate had only been known to the locals as being a loud mouth pro-slavery newspaper man from Westport.

"Ya better watch yer step now, tho'," claimed the man who was dusting himself off and rubbing one sore elbow. "Clay Pate has been appointed a Ew-nited States Marshall and he can do as he pleases with you bunch o' Free-Staters."

"Yeah," chimed in one of the other men. "We all heard about

how some of ya'll butchered our friends and Pate is determined to do sumpthin' 'bout it, too.

"We already got one of yer people," he went on, "a man by th' name of Moore that claims to be a preacher. We'll get the rest of the information we need from that old man and then there'll really be hell to pay."

It was determined that these were the three men that had recently raided a Palmyra farm house and made off with some guns and provisions after half wrecking the place.

The two Moore boys demanded that they make an attempt to rescue their father immediately. Rev. William Moore and four or five sons had been among the first to settle in Franklin County near Norwood in 1854.

Before replying, Brown had the three Missourians taken prisoner and turned over to Captain Shore who detailed some men to guard them.

"We can't go running off in the middle of the day," said Brown as he gathered his men off to one side. "I'm certain we will be outnumbered and they'll spot us coming before we can be ready."

Pausing, Brown looked at Shore and said, "You get your men together and we'll head for Black Jack late this afternoon so we can be ready to attack at first light tomorrow. There is a new moon tonight so we will have the cover of near darkness to help us get in position without being seen."

The men were called together and given instructions as to exactly how they were to proceed to be certain each person understood what was about to take place the following morning. This was not to be just a mob of men charging into a fight.

"We are a militia, not a posse or a gang. Pate has access to cannon, but I have no idea if he has them with him or if so, intends to use them when discovered," said Captain Brown. "We will divide unto groups and I'll direct you to your positions when we see how

148

well Pate is organized; that is if it has occurred to him to do more than just roam the countryside with his bunch of bushwhackers. I doubt if he expects the type of fight we are prepared to give him."

Brown paced back and forth, his piercing blue eyes falling on each man. There was dedication and determination in his voice that was transferred to each man under his command.

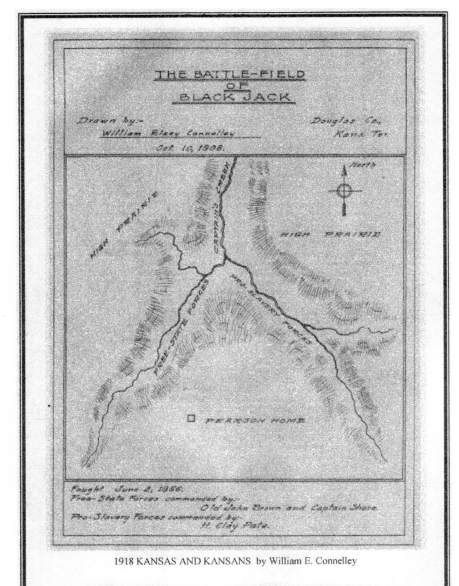

1918 KANSAS AND KANSANS by William E. Connelley

BLACK JACK BATTLEFIELD
June 2, 1856

Chapter 25

Sunday night, June 1st, 1856

Brown and Shore's company amounted at first to around forty men. However a few of the less enthusiastic dropped out during the night as the company headed for Black Jack.

Arriving around midnight Brown, who had been given the title of Captain, spotted a small grove of trees on what seemed like an endless prairie. They estimated they were a little over a mile and a half to the west of Black Jack.

Brown was definitely in command. There were still some hints of hesitation in some of the men, even Captain Shore himself.

The plan was for Brown and his men to be in the center and right with Shore's men to spread out on the left flank. Brown told his young son Fred to stay with the horses while Shore detailed five of his men to do the same. Redpath also observed from this vantage point.

Abrael stood looking first at Brown and then at Weiner. He wanted desperately to join the group heading for the creek but was certain he too would be instructed to remain with the horses.

Weiner spotted Abrael's questioning look, then motioned with a nod of his head for Abrael to follow closely behind him.

"Us Jew boys gotta stick together, and you look as ready as any of us," said Weiner.

Abrael quickly dropped the horses' reigns, grabbed his rifle and anxiously fell in behind Weiner and Bondi. This was going to be his fight. He had decided this was to be his land, his home and he was ready for whatever the cost!

Ahead of them was the west branch of Captain's Creek, along the bank of which, and in the deep ruts of the Santa Fe Trail, Brown and his men would take a stand.

As dawn was about to break, Pate's camp could be seen on the hill just above the east branch of Captain's Creek. Although his wagons were in a semi circle they seemed almost casually placed, rather than designed to provide cover. It was as if they never considered or cared if they were discovered. Rather than behind them, their horses were off to their right

By now Brown's men numbered just over two dozen. There was Brown, his sons Owen, Frederick (watching the horses), Oliver, Salmon and Watson along with son-in-law Henry Thompson, Dr. Westfall, Weiner, Bondi, Kepper, the two Moore's, Charlie Kaiser, Ben Cochrane, George Rowe and James Townsley who was still somewhat uncertain, Shore and his men and the volunteers who were out on the left flank.

Several men had the Sharp's rifles. It was awkward for Abrael. He was not a weapons man but he knew they were fortunate to have more than a few who were. He remembered that Rev. Beecher had said that the rifles were needed by the Kansans because "you might as well read the Bible to a buffalo as to get Atchison and Stringfellow to listen to reason".

Abrael had fumbled with the small caps that were the primers for the rifle. He would lose them in his pocket and drop them in the grass. He decided to depend on the pistol in his belt more as the action started and they got within small arms range.

As if caused by the snap of a finger it seemed to be daylight. Brown yelled, "Follow me," and started at a run down the hill toward the creek. Rifle fire broke out from the Missourian's side although ineffectual due to the distance. Brown was surprised that Pate had set pickets out around his perimeter. He gave Pate little credit for knowing much about military organization or tactics.

Brown's men had been ordered not to fire until they were in sufficient range and had found what cover they could in the ruts and tall prairie grass. Brown was painfully aware that not only were they badly out numbered but that their ammunition was in very short supply.

Brown looked around to see Captain Shore close by but many of Shore's men had remained atop the hill wasting some of that valuable ammunition that was falling far short of Pate's position. Soon more of Shore's men had left. Brown had no idea just how many men he had left but his determination could not be dampened.

Abrael took his place to the right of Weiner which put him then on the far flank. He measured the space between himself and Weiner and decided he could cover the distance easily, firing from about four positions making it seem like there were several shooters in his immediate area.

1855 and 1856 had been the driest years folks could remember. There hadn't even been much snow but this morning the tall prairie grass was still wet with dew. The grass blades were sharp and Abrael knew he would soon be covered with the tiny no-see-em's that would cause him to itch all day. And there were ticks to worry about.

"Ticks to worry about," Abrael whispered to himself. "Now's a fine time for me to be worrying about ticks and such. Bullets are gonna be a lot more worrisome in a minute, I'll bet."

"What's that?" asked Weiner, as he peered through the weeds.

"I said that the grass was wet," replied Abrael.

"Gee, you got a lot o' troubles besides just bein' a Jew, ain't cha?"

For an instant Abrael didn't see the grin on Weiner's face. Abrael was caught off guard because generally Weiner was not a joking man.

For some unknown reason Pate and some of his men had left the concealment of the circled wagons and raced down their side of the east branch of the creek and lay on the bank nearest Brown's position. Firing from a semi prone position they could be seen hunkered down in the prairie grasses and rain gullies that coursed toward the creek bed. The two groups were about eighty yards apart.

"How many of 'em do ya think there are?" asked one of Pate's men.

"How do I know? They're keepin' their heads down, which is what I suggest you do."

"Just about the time I get ready to nail one of 'em, he's gone and another pops up next to 'em."

Just prior to the first shots Brown had instructed his men; "They must have us out numbered two…three to one. We can't let them know that there are so few of us.

"Don't waste ammunition but keep firing. Just move to one side or the other each time you fire. We'll try to make them think there are more of us than there are."

"He's tryin' to make them to think there is a whole army over here," Abrael said to Weiner. "Think we can do it?"

"Make some noise if ya' can but stay down," was Weiner's reply. "If we can make each shot count, that'll give them enough to worry about."

The firing was constant from Brown's side of the creek. His men would call out to one another using different names as if there were twice as many as they actually were.

Shore's men increased their firing from behind as Brown and his men raced down the side of the hill toward the old Santa Fe Trail ruts. Soon off to Brown's right there was firing first from Weiner and then Bondi. Off to Brown's left came more sporadic fire. Abrael fired in the direction of Pate's camp, not knowing if he would be able to hit anyone, then rolled several times to his right, reloaded and fired at a dark object crouching below one of the Missourian's wagons. He heard a curse but had no idea if his bullet had hit its mark or not.

Just then a ball showered Abrael's face with dirt and grass causing his eyes to water. At first Abrael thought he was bleeding but discovered it was just perspiration running down his forehead.

A rifle ball smacked and splintered a board on the side of one of Pate's wagons causing the rifleman just below it to scramble backwards and behind the wooden wheel.

A scream was heard from one of the Missourians as dust puffed up from the shoulder of his jacket.

"Hey," cried one of Pate's men, "they're all up and down the creek and in the trail ruts." Just then dirt exploded in his eyes and he fell back clawing at his face and dropping his rifle. As the rifle hit the ground it went off almost striking Pate's boot.

"Keep your eyes sharp. They're firing from everywhere over there," called out Pate.

Just then Pate heard a squeal and a voice from one of Brown's men cried out "gotcha, damn ya." He wondered which of his men had been hit.

Brown concentrated his fire upon the puffs of smoke from the other side of the creek. Pates men were trying to stay in position behind the wagons and on the bank of the creek.

Abrael saw one of Pate's men jump to his feet and head for a group of horses just behind and off to the right of their wagons. He had taken about three steps when one leg went out from under him and he sprawled in the dirt clutching at his wound.

Suddenly a cry went up from Brown's side. It was his son-in-law Henry Thompson. Brown could see a spreading crimson blotch on the front of Henry's shirt. Dr. Westfall rushed to Henry's side and helped him first to his knees and then to his feet. Trying to crouch and move at the same time the two men staggered back to where the horses were being held. The wound was serious and had to be dealt with immediately.

"Watch your selves," cried Brown. "Keep low and move... move...ya hear?"

Soon another cry went up and Abrael saw Carpenter, who had been acting more or less as their guide, grabbed at his face. The end of his nose had been shot off and the bullet had gone on into his shoulder causing him to struggle to the rear.

Almost as in response, a cry rang out from one of Pate's men as he felt the burn of a rifle ball along his left ribs.

"The boys are gittin' hungry, Capt'n. I better head off and git 'em somethin' t' eat." Brown neither replied to Shore nor did he look up. Shore was soon gone. Close on Shore's heels, Townsley announced that he was going for more ammunition. He too disappeared from the battlefield.

Brown moved back and forth checking on each of his men. Gathering Weiner, Bondi and the two Moore boys he said, "I think we have them convinced that we have the capacity to take them. I have seen several of Pate's men crawling backwards and disappearing behind their wagons."

"And I saw a couple grab their horses and skedaddle back toward the east," said one of the Moore's.

"We can't let them get away. We must stop them somehow." Brown paused and then said, "When I say ready and wave my hat, you men follow me up the side of that hill." He pointed to a spot just south of Pate's camp.

Abrael dropped his rifle, pulled his pistol from his belt and jumped to his feet. As he ran he tried wiping the dampness from the weapon.

At that same instant Brown began to run down the hill, hesitated after about twenty feet and waved; the rest followed and met up with Brown at the bottom of the hill ready to proceed.

Brown motioned to the two Moore boys, "I want you to shoot their horses and mules. We can't let them get away from us now. Remember;" he said emphatically, "just the animals. I don't want any more men killed or hurt if we can help it." With four shots the Moore's brought down two mules and two horses.

Abrael, upon hearing Captain Brown's words about needless

killing thought back to just a few nights ago when this same man stood by while five pro-slavery men, the same as the Missourians in front of him, were slaughtered in a much more brutal manner than just being shot by an enemy with whom they could fight back. Brown had said just before they had made their way to Pottawamie, "an eye for an eye". Now several of his men had been wounded; Henry could easily die from his chest wound, and yet Brown called for no more unnecessary killing of his sworn enemy. It was puzzlement to the young Jew.

Suddenly they heard a wild whoop. Abrael immediately crouched down expecting a charge from the Missourians; then was the first to look up to his right and see a horseman racing up between the two creeks. The horse was wild-eyed as the rider smashed his heels into the horse's flanks. The rider waved his sword above his head making his mount even wilder.

"Yeeeeehaw.......we got 'em. We got 'em surrounded. Yaaaaaha!"

It was Brown's son Frederick. He had left the horses and was now charging into the middle of the battle. It was never known whether it was a brilliant idea on his part or one of his mental lapses that were by now common in the young lad. Brown never asked the boy.

For a moment shots continued to ring out and then Brown, recognizing his son, yelled for his men to stop shooting.

The shooting from the Missourian's side, whether from surprise or fear, stopped also. Seeing Redpath following Frederick at a distance, Pate was certain they were about to face reinforcements for this bunch of Free-Staters. This was more then he had bargained for. He was after Brown not some local militia and now he was in danger of being beaten without accomplishing his original mission.

"I'll find that Brown and his little band of killers if I have to cover every acre of this country," he had told his men. "And now," he thought to himself, "I get ambushed by a force that think they are a militia equal to ours. Who are they and where did they come from?"

If there were reinforcements behind yonder hill, this "little militia" would put a stop to Pate's hunt for Brown or any thing else, and Pate now realized it.

Chapter 26

Convinced he was out numbered and out gunned Pate decided his only option was to try to call some kind of truce. He was certain in his mind at the time that his position as a U. S. Marshall and commander of an authorized Missouri Militia would be enough leverage to cause what must be a Free-State militia to bring this battle to an end. Pate had many more wounded than he cared to acknowledge and he too was aware that many of his Missourians had fled at the sign, however false, of Free-State reinforcements.

Pate selected a Mr. James and a Free-State prisoner by the name of Lymer to present a white flag of truce and ask for a conference with who ever was in charge of the Free-Staters.

As Abrael kept his pistol trained in Brown's direction, Brown moved toward the men carrying the flag of truce.

"Are you in command of that group?" asked Captain Brown to Lymer; knowing full well he was not.

"No Sir," said Lymer. "But…"

"I will speak with no one other than the Commander," stated Brown. With that, leaving Mr. James with Brown, Lymer returned to where Pate was observing the confrontation.

"He won't talk to anyone but you Captain,' said Lymer.

With that Pate strode down the hill. The sun told them it was an hour or so past noonday.

Brown began by asking if Pate had a proposition to make. "Definitely not! You see, Sir," began Pate, "I am United States Marshal H. Clay Pate and Captain of this authorized Missouri Militia. I trust that…"

"I know who you are," said Brown in a deep, firm voice that could be heard throughout the valley.

Pate was suddenly aware just who this tall determined man was.

His heart sank as he realized what he would later relate as he told of this event, "I went to take Old Brown and Old Brown took me".

"Well," said Brown, "I have a proposition to make to you. And that is full and unconditional surrender." With that Brown raised his pistol and held it near Pate's head. The matter appeared to all concerned to be settled.

Pate, seeing he had little choice, agreed. He turned and walked with Brown up the hill to his command headquarters. Brown had ordered his men to gather the Missourians together to prevent escape and to collect their weapons. Brown himself had relieved Pate of all his weapons including a long shining Bowie knife that would one day become the model for another of Brown's weapons for freedom.

At first, Lieutenant W. B. Brocket, second in command of the Missourians, appeared to be ready to continue the fight despite Pate's surrender.

"It's done," said Pate in a firm but quiet voice. "Have all the men lay down their weapons."

There were a little over twenty able bodied men to relinquish their weapons and form in a group surrounded by Brown's meager force which by this time numbered less than two dozen. Some of Pate's men looked around wondering where the rest of the Free-Staters were.

Abrael moved about the Missourian's wagons and watched the wounded being cared for. It appeared that more than half a dozen had been pretty severely wounded and it was evident that well over a dozen had fled during the battle.

One of the first things done was to retrieve the three prisoners the Missourians had taken which included the Moore boys' father, shaken but unharmed. He told of being held down the night before while a pint of liquor was forced down his throat. Laughing and drinking themselves the Missourian thought that was great sport.

The Missourians had brought with them several wagons of supplies, including food, tents, rifles, pistols and much ammunition. This was a very welcome sight to Brown's men having been short on everything for several days. All of this was gathered together along with the prisoners, two wagons and teams, close to twenty-five saddle horses and then herded toward Prairie City.

Shortly after the surrender The Lawrence Stubbs group and Major Abbott arrived along with several others, including the other New York reporter W. A. Phillips, followed at a distance by both Shore and Townsley.

"Yer not gonna like this," said Shore. He had pulled Old Brown off to one side. "They done got both Jason and John Jr.," he said turning away so the others might not hear.

"Are they alive? Are they alright?" questioned Brown in a loud voice.

Both Abrael and August heard Brown and started toward the two men.

"Well, answer me!" said Brown loudly as he grabbed shore's shirt front.

"I go no idea. I just heard it in town. Happened yestidy er th' day b'fore. Heard they was sendin' 'em to Tecumseh. That must mean ther're alive at least."

Men, supplies, wagons and weapons were taken together to Prairie City close to Brown's camp on Ottawa Creek. To Brown's credit the first thing that was done was to call for a meal to be fixed. The women of the small village went to work after cooking fires were prepared and using the supplies brought from Pate's camp made a meal sufficient for everyone. Brown's men suddenly realized how hungry they were having had their last meal the day before. No doubt Pate and his men had a good supper the night before the battle.

"Looks like we're finally going to get to eat," said Abrael to

Townsley. Townsley didn't look up as he replied in a low voice, "Yeah. Guess so."

"I didn't realize how hungry I was," went on Abrael. "I suppose it was all the excitement.

"Heard how Henry's doin'?" continued Abrael.

"Yeah," replied Townsley. "Doc says he's lucky as hell but he'll live okay."

"Hope Carpenter's gonna be okay without the end of his nose." Townsley shrugged.

"I know it's not funny but at least he can say he was hit in front and not in back."

"Just what's that supposed t' mean," glared Townsley at Abrael. "If'n you got somthin' t' say, say it."

"I didn't mean anything by it at all," replied Abrael. "Come on let's get something to eat. I'm starved."

Townsley looked at Abrael, turned from the cook fire and slowly walked away; not going near the food that was waiting.

After the meal was finished, Brown being the very last to eat, the camp was organized. Moving to a grove on the banks of Ottawa Creek not too far from Prairie City guards were chosen so the prisoners could be made secure. Most of the men in Brown's group were anxious to return home to their work and to be certain their families had remained safe. There were so few of Brown's people left that even Old Brown took a turn guarding the Missourians.

The following morning with the help of The Lawrence Stubbs and others that began to arrive to help, more organization took place. A fortress of a sort was quickly constructed using the creek banks and trenches that were dug by Brown's, Shore's and Captain McWhinney's men.

"'Camp Brown' I heard someone call it," exclaimed Abrael as he sat down to rest after piling up some dead logs along the dirt bank.

"Guess that'll do," said August Bondi, wiping the sweat from his forehead.

"You met my friend Luke, Abrael?" asked Bondi. "As a matter of fact, we just met ourselves."

"Luke, this here is another one of our little group Abrael Kepper. He's been working some with Weiner at the store but what he really wants is to be a teacher."

"We're gonna need all those we can get around here," said Luke as he reached down and shook Abrael's hand.

"Well, it's my turn for guard duty fellas, see you later." With that August pulled together his ragged clothing and headed for the area where the captives were being held.

No personal items had been taken from any of the prisoners and they had been allowed to make use of their own blankets and tents. It was odd that Brown's people had to 'borrow' some of the blankets belonging to the Missourians because Pate's men had stolen and destroyed all that Brown had at one of his sons' a week or so before. However they had not found Brown there.

Even Pate admitted later that, as prisoners, they had been treated well, even though he continued to argue that he was taken against the common practice accepted of truce under a white flag.

Brown summoned Abrael and Fred Brown. "Fred, you take Oliver and three of the other's and head for Centropolis and get clothing for some of these men. Many are in rags and can hardly keep themselves covered. Nothing fancy understand and just what we need to get by. Later we'll make it right with them somehow."

Brown turned to Abrael and asked him to write up an agreement that would state the terms of surrender and prisoner exchange that Pate and Brown had agreed upon.

To be held on neutral ground, it was to be a case of one for one; with Brown Sr.'s two sons, Captain John Jr. and Jason Brown to be first exchanged for Captain H. C. Pate and Lieutenant W. B. Brocket.

It was not learned until later how badly John Jr. had been treated when captured with his brother. He had been forced to trot for ten miles ahead of his mounted captors with his hands tied tightly behind his back then tortured during their captivity.

And John Brown Sr. had not had his full revenge yet. That would come another day soon!

Chapter 27

Governor Shannon had become very alarmed at the news of the Battle of Black Jack and even published a wide sweeping proclamation on June 4th demanding the immediate dispersion of all armed, illegal organizations. These ranged from those calling themselves Kansas Militia, Bloomington Rifles, Blue Mound Infantry, Prairie City Company and many others choosing names to make them sound official.

Fifty Federal Dragoons under the command of Colonel Edwin Vose Sumner, a veteran of the Black Hawk War and the Mexican war was immediately sent from Lecompton on June 5th to separate the hostiles concentrated near Palmyra at Brown's camp. His orders were to take charge of Brown's twenty-six prisoners, free them and assist the Marshall to carry out what writs they had with them for the arrest of fugitives named in those writs; some of whom were reported to be among Brown's militia.

As the Colonel approached the Brown camp, which was highly visible on the open prairie, Brown accompanied by August Bondi, made a big deal out of meeting with the Commander under the proper and formal procedures. Colonel Sumner made it clear that he wasn't dealing formally with a bunch of lawless men. After receiving that message from the Colonel, Brown Sr. and Shore rode back out to meet the anxiously waiting army.

Sumner stated in plain language his orders and insisted they be carried out immediately. Marshall Fain searched his pockets and finally found his packet of papers and reported that apparently there was no one in the present company listed on any of his writs.

It is suggested that Sumner took Brown Sr. aside and said that there was a warrant out for his arrest but that it must have been lost or left at Lecompton.

While everyone seemed to be milling around watching Col. Sumner trying to gain some semblance of order between Brown, Pate and the men with rifles pointing in all directions, Salmon Brown picked up his loaded double-barreled shot gun by the muzzle, lost his grip and let the gun hit the ground.

Abrael almost jumped out of his skin as the shotgun discharged and Salmon let out a scream. The shot had torn into his upper arm tearing the muscle badly. The men closest to him quickly carried him to Carter's cabin, August following closely behind.

Abrael was waiting just outside the cabin door while Dr. Westfall treated the wound. "How's he doin'?"

"He'll be all right," replied Bondi, "but I'm going to stay with him a day or two just in case. The Doc said he would be around tomorrow just to be sure. You'd better go on and let them know where I am."

"If there is anything I can do to help," said Abrael, "just send for me."

Chapter 28

Heading back to where Old Brown and Colonel Sumner were still talking, Abrael noticed a young lieutenant sitting a beautiful horse. Most horses belonging to the Army Dragoons were much more common in appearance and performance. The lieutenant saw Abrael admiring the animal and moved in his direction.

"Abrael Kepper is my name," said Abrael as he laid one hand gently on the horse's neck and offered the other to the lieutenant. "You don't see this fine an animal in the Army very often."

"This one goes with me everywhere I go. He is my own personal mount; brought him all the way from Laurel Hill in Virginia. That's where my home is." The smiling lieutenant extended his hand to Abrael and said, "Lieutenant J. E. B. Stuart, your servant Sir.

"I hope you don't mind me saying that I believe I hear a slight Jewish accent in your voice. I take it you aren't from around here either."

"You're right but actually I am from here; at least I am now. I came here from Missouri on my way from New Port, Rhode Island. I came to Missouri in '47 and here two years ago. And I caught your accent from back east too, Lieutenant."

"I have only been here for a short time," said the lieutenant, "and most people call me Jeb."

"I hope this has not caused you a lot of trouble but I am certainly glad to see you," stated Abrael. "I'm not certain the fighting is over even yet. I understand there is a large group of proslavery militia over at Bull Creek east of Palmyra and it is said that the free-staters are gathering their companies and heading that way too. It's going to be bigger that Black Jack if they find each other."

"You people are really serious about the slavery business here in the Kansas Territory aren't you? Frankly I think the Army's biggest problem, is going to be the Cheyennes out West. They are anxious for a fight and I am afraid we will be in for one soon."

"Everyone is trying to make a home for themselves I guess."

"That why you're here?" asked Stuart.

"Good a place as any. My people have been looking for a long time and this is one place we haven't tried yet. Sure hope we can get this settled and get on with building up to Statehood."

Lieutenant Stuart placed both hands on his saddle horn and leaned forward, looking off toward the West. "You know unless you have lived with slavery most people don't really understand it. All they can imagine is black folks in chains and being worked to death. Tell me Abrael, would you treat your team of horses or mules that way?"

"Well...," said Abrael haltingly.

"Of course not; oh, sometimes you must discipline an animal until it learns the best way to do its work. The same is true with people. But keeping the help healthy and providing for their needs just makes things better for everyone; and more productive too."

"I see your line of thinking Leiut...ah...Jeb, but you are forgetting a couple of very important things. You're forgetting about the forced separation of families and especially about freedom. Freedom Lieutenant! And you're forgetting about being considered second class or sometimes even no class at all. You see..., being a Jew, I know all about that."

Before the lieutenant could reply Colonel Sumner was calling his Dragoons into formation and preparing to leave. Stuart smiled, gave a quick salute and cantered back to his unit. Just then Captain Pate found an empty wagon bed, climbed atop and began what he intended to be an oration fitting for the time and situation.

"I feel compelled to clarify and even rectify the impressions that have been assumed here in so far as we of the proslavery persuasion have been........."

"I don't want to hear another word out of you, Sir." thundered Colonel Sumner – "not a word, Sir! You have no business here. The Governor told me so!"

Red faced and flustered Pate slowly moved to the ground, then straightened himself and strode defiantly toward a group of his men.

The prisoners had been ordered released and told to leave immediately. Those at Camp Sackett would be dealt with in due time according to the Colonel. Right now he had more pressing matters with which to attend. As he formed his men he remembered that Governor Shannon had commented that if they had taken steps six months ago to try to disband these local militias they probably would have been able to bring these situations to an end.

"As for me," muttered the Colonel, "I damn well doubt it. I think this is just the beginning."

THE BEGINNING!

AFTERWORD

Friday, June 6, 1856

Historical records tell us that Jacob Cantrell did have troubles with the Missourians ever since he left that State sometime in 1854. He had been threatened and hunted and had done his best to keep his family from harm in their new home hoping the freedom of the Territory would help protect them

He became afraid the Missourians would attack his home along with the others that had been either threatened or rumored to be on *"their list"*. His wife Rebecca was also afraid but did not try to talk him out of taking his place along with the others headed for the Black Jack battle.

"Thought we didn't know you were with the Browns, did ya'?" grinned Pate as he stood in the door to Cantrell's cabin several days after the battle. Jacob had left immediately when the surrender was about to take place but apparently had been recognized by one of the Missourians.

"Tell yer wife you've got a trip to make and be quick about it."

At Bull Creek, Pate and his men made camp for the night. Cantrell was kept secured and put *"on trial"* for treason against Missouri the next morning.

"Can't be no other verdict than guilty," said Pate. "And you know the penalty!"

Three shots very slowly rang out.

"Remind you of anything?" Pate said glaring down at Cantrell's body. "Those were our friends at Pottawatomie. I guess two can play at that game!"[10]

And so they did; all the way to Fort Sumter!

---

10 No one was ever tried or convicted for the murder of Jacob Cantrell.

Concerning the Massacre

It would seem that the actions of John Brown at Pottawatomie and Black Jack caused first Buford and his men then other Missourians to pause and reflect on the apparent determination of the Free-Staters.

After the capture of the three pro-slavery forts, Franklin, Saunders and Titus which had been designed to starve out the Free-Staters of Lawrence, and the formation of Lane's and Montgomery's armies, the growing numbers of Free-Staters began to take heart. They believed they had a chance for peace and a free state. They now had and showed the confidence needed to make their dreams come true.

The resignation of the first three Democratic Governors; Andrew Reeder, Wilson Shannon and six-foot six John White Geary, caused by their unwillingness to force the President's pro-slavery demands on the Kansans, added strength to the belief that the free-State cause could be realized.

Comments made later concerning the "Pottawamie Massacre"

Wrote Governor Charles Robinson, February, 1878

"I never had much doubt that Capt. Brown was the author of the blow at Pottawamie, for the reason that he was the only man who comprehended the situation, and saw the absolute necessity of some such blow and had the nerve to strike it."

Judge Hanway, statement of February 1, 1878, accurately summarizes the progress of public opinion in the neighborhood of the crime;

"…so far as public opinion in the neighborhood, where the affair took place, is concerned, I believe I may state that public opinion was considerably divided; but after the whole circumstances became known, there was a reaction in public opinion and the Free State settlers who had claims on the creek considered that Capt. Brown and his party of eight had performed a justifiable act, which saved their homes and dwellings from threatened raids of the proslavery party."

Thomas Wentworth Higginson, in his 'Cheerful Yesterdays' states;

"In regard to the most extreme act of John Brown's Kansas career, the so-called 'Pottawatomie massacre' of May 24, 1856, I can testify that in September of that year, there appeared to be but one way of thinking among the Kansas Free State men…I heard of no one who did not approve of the act, and its beneficial effects were universally asserted Governor Robinson himself fully endorsing it to me…"

"…Two officers were standing off to one side listening to Elias tell about John Brown.

"He won, you know."

"What you mean he won?" questioned the other. "He got a bayonet in him and then they hung him."

"That's all right, he still won. Everybody up and down the East Coast heard about Old John Brown and what he did and why he did it. You know Captain, those easterners are the ones that had the money, but it was Old John Brown…, Old Captain Brown that had the nerve. No, Old Captain Brown won alright."[11]

---

11   From **"The Chance"** by *Dale E. Vaughn*

Other books by *Dale E. Vaughn*

"The Chance"

The very first black troops to fight in uniform during the American Civil War were the 1st Kansas Colored Volunteer Infantry. Formed in 1862 this heroic group of soldiers suffered among the highest casualties of any unit as they battled the Confederates and Indians in Kansas, Oklahoma, Indian Territory and Arkansas. A gripping historically factual novel about comradeship, hardship, suffering and a quest for freedom. (*Available from book stores or from the Author – e-mail* nandale@networksplus.net)

"His Way

Conversations with Jesus; not bringing Him down to our level but *into* our level. Discovering how much fun He is to visit with and to learn from when dealing with the problems *and* the joys of our daily lives. What a Guy - What a God. (*Available only by contacting the author.*)

------- Coming Soon -------

"Buyin' The Farm"

In 1861, seventeen year old J.T. Morris wants his parents and himself out of the coal mines of Virginia and on to a farm in Kansas Territory but a Pony Express conspiracy and the Civil War put danger in his way.

"Big Boy - Little Boy"

J. T. Morris returns to Virginia to get his family only to find his old home deserted and a young nephew waiting for him. The Civil War has taken its toll and drags JT deeper into dangerous circumstances in a war that he claims "is not my fight".

"Little Cheat"
What Ever It Takes

Elias Mothers, veteran of the 1st Kansas Colored Vol. Infantry, sets out in the final months of the American Civil War to find his little brother Cheat who had gone missing while Elias was away. Elias discovers that his fight for freedom did little to change the way he and his people are treated; and that heroes seem to run in the Mothers' family.

LaVergne, TN USA
30 June 2010
187812LV00003B/4/P